Storybook Treasury

Storybook Treasury

Baker Books

A Division of Baker Book House Co
Grand Rapids, Michigan 49516

Art © 1979, 1981, 1988 by Samuel J. Butcher Company
Text © 1969, 1987 by Baker Books, ©1988 by Samuel J. Butcher Company

Published by Baker Books
a division of Baker Book House Company
P.O. Box 6287, Grand Rapids, MI 49516-6287

Printed in the United States of America

New combined edition published 2000. Previously published as *Precious Moments Stories from the Bible* by Sheri Haan and *Precious Moments Bedtime Stories* by Samuel J. and Jon Butcher, Debbie Ann and Craig Wiersma.

ISBN 0-8010-4458-8

Library of Congress Cataloging-in-Publication Data is on file at the Library of Congress, Washington, DC.

For current information about all releases from Baker Book House, visit our web site:
http://www.bakerbooks.com

Contents

6

God Makes
the World

Nothing at All

(Genesis 1:2)

When you were playing today,
what did you see?
   a furry kitten?
      a busy ant?
      Maybe you saw
         children playing.

13

If it was warm,
you might have
seen a fuzzy flower,
a beautiful butterfly,
or some buzzing bees.

Perhaps you
played outside.

If it was very cold you might have rolled in the snow and made angels. Maybe you went ice-skating. Isn't it fun to see, hear, and smell all the beautiful things God made for us?

Did you know that long, long ago there were no trees or flowers? No children played in the sunshine or in the snow. In fact, there was nothing at all. Everywhere it was empty and dark. God and His angels were the only living beings. They were living in heaven.

Maybe you wonder how the world got

here. Just keep reading, and you'll find the story of God making His lovely world.

Day and Night

(Genesis 1:3–5)

On the first day God divided the day from the night.

God often walked through the darkness and emptiness. One day He had something very special in mind as He looked around Him. God decided to make the world.

You may think that this would be impossible to do because there was nothing for God to use. There was no lumber, bricks, or cement. Everywhere it was black and still. But you must remember that God can do all things. That is why it was not difficult for God. The only thing He said was, "Let there be light."

As soon as God spoke, the darkness began to move. Light began to show where darkness had been. The darkness and the light kept moving until they were separated. It was no longer black everywhere because God had made light.

God looked at what He had made and He liked it very much. God said that He would call the light, day. The darkness He called night. That was the first day.

Heaven and Earth

(Genesis 1:6–8)

On the second day God looked at what He had made the day before, the day and the night. He was happy with it. But today He had something else on His mind. He was going to make the earth and sky.

The second day God made sky and earth.

God spoke. He said that the sky should be over the earth. And from nowhere the sky began to move together and the earth came together. When it was finished, the sky was above the earth just like God wanted it to be. God said that He would call the sky, heaven. That was the end of the second day. Now there was day and night and heaven and earth. Again God was very pleased with what He had made—all of it out of nothing.

Land and Water

(Genesis 1:9–13)

Dry land appeared on the third day.

In the morning of the third day God came to the world He was making. As He looked at it, He knew that He wasn't finished. There were so many

19

things He wanted to make. But on this day He was going to make the land and the water.

Just as before, God spoke. This time He said that all the water should come together and stay by itself. The land should be by itself and it should be dry land.

As the land moved together God put green grass on it. He also put gardens and trees on the land. Some of the trees were tall and thin. Others were short and fat like bushes. God put blossoms and fruit on some of these trees. The world was beginning to look more like God wanted it to look.

Even the water was now alone. Some of it was put in very large places. These were the oceans and the seas. Some of the water ran in wide, deep streams and rivers. The tiny moving brooks came, too. You can almost hear the music that the waters were making. The waves of the large oceans slapped on the shores. The little streams made high tinkling sounds as they trickled down the sides of the rocks.

God looked at the land and the water. His world looked more beautiful every day. The morning and the evening of the third day were over.

Skylights

(Genesis 1:14–19)

On the fourth day God made the sun, moon, and stars.

As God came to the world on the fourth day He knew just what He would do. He wanted to make lights for the sky. This is how we tell day from night and why we have days, weeks, and years. This is how we tell time.

God said that the sun should be the light of the day. Immediately the big, round, hot sun came into the sky and made the day look alive. The green of the plants was brighter. The sun made the quiet water look like a giant mirror. The sun warmed everything it could touch. It helped the gardens grow strong and green.

For the night God made another light. It is the moon. It's the bigger light that you see in the sky at night. It is the light you often look for if your bedroom seems too dark. There are other little lights in the sky. They are the stars that play hide-and-seek with you when you are in bed.

When God had finished this, the night of the fourth day came, and all was dark and still, but the stars were shining.

Perch and Peacocks

(Genesis 1:20–23)

The fish and birds appeared on the fifth day.

The world that God had made looked very beautiful. Trees and flowers sprouted and bloomed. There were glowing lights in the sky, and the waters were shades of blue and gray-green.

But in the air and water there was nothing living yet. So God spoke and soon the oceans and seas were filled with whales, porpoises, clams, and starfish. The lakes were full of perch, pike, bluegills, bass, crabs, and turtles. Trout began to swim in the streams.

God spoke to fill the air with colorful birds. Some of the birds were strong and flew many miles without stopping. Others could fly, but weren't so strong. They stayed closer to the earth and perched in the bushes and on the lower branches of the trees. God gave the birds feathery coats of rainbow colors.

You can imagine the wonderful sights God must have seen on the evening of this day. The sun began to tuck itself behind the hills. The birds came to their perches to roost for the night. God looked at all these things He had made on the fifth day. He was glad He had made them.

Man and Animals
(Genesis 1:24–28)

As God walked about His world on the morning of the sixth day, He knew that

He would soon be finished. There were living things in the sea and in the air. But there was nothing living on the ground.

God looked over the world and said that animals should be made and that they should have babies. Then God made the animals of every size, shape, and color you can think of. Some were as tall as the giraffe and the dinosaur. They munched leaves from the highest branches. The squirrels and the monkeys were smaller but quicker. They could turn and scamper away as they teased the zebras. God liked all the animals He had made.

Even after the animals had been made, God was not finished. There was no one to take care of the animals and the gardens.

There was no one at all who could help them. So God said that He would make a man who would be very much like God Himself.

God took some of the dust from the ground. He worked with it until He had made the man exactly as He wanted him. But before man would be complete, God had to breathe a breath of air into him so he could live.

On the sixth day God made man.

Now the animals had a friend to care for them. Man was much different from everything else God had made. Man had a soul. That means that he could speak, think, and love. God and man often talked together. God told the man that it was his job to take care of this lovely world.

Finally the daylight began to dim. The moon peeked over the mountains. It climbed higher and higher until it joined the stars. The sixth day was over. God was pleased because everything He had made was very good.

God Rests

(Genesis 2:1–3)

On the seventh morning God came to His world but He did not work. He did not make anything at all. The Bible tells us that God rested on the seventh day. That is the very reason that we are supposed to rest and praise God on one day of the week.

God rested on the seventh day.

As God rested He must have listened to

the sounds of his world. The fish splashed water as they played in the lakes. The birds chirped and laughed as they watched

the animals below running through the grasses. Some of the animals napped, and God could hear the sounds of sleep. Even the humming of the song birds could be heard as God rested.

Now you know the story of God's world and how He made all of it out of nothing. When you see and hear the sights and sounds of God's world, sing to Him and thank Him for all these good things He made.

The World
Becomes Sinful

A Lovely Home

(Genesis 2:8–9, 15–17)

God made a special place for Adam. It was called the Garden of Eden. There were so many beautiful plants and trees in it. God knew that it would be a pleasant place for Adam to live. There were rivers flowing through it and there were many precious stones. The Garden of Eden must have looked even lovelier than the most colorful and well-kept park you have ever

seen. God brought Adam to this garden and told him that it would be his home. He should care for it and give names to every bird, plant, and animal.

Before God left, He had something very important to say. God told Adam about the many different trees He had made. Adam could see the fruit on some of these trees. It looked so ripe and juicy. God said that he could eat any fruit from these trees except from one. That was the Tree of Knowledge of Good and Evil. God explained to him that if he should ever eat even one piece of fruit from this tree, he would be sinning and would die. Eating from the tree would be sin because it would be disobeying God. After God finished speaking, He left Adam in the garden by himself.

A Wife for Adam

(Genesis 2:18, 21–25)

Taking care of God's new world would be a big task. Adam might need some help. There were many animals and birds, but they couldn't help Adam. They could not talk to him and keep him company. God didn't want Adam to feel lonely. So God made Adam fall sound asleep. Then God took one of Adam's ribs, one of the bones from his chest. From this bone, God made a woman and gave her a soul.

Adam and Eve must have talked together about all of the beauty around them. They enjoyed being together. They loved to sing and laugh. They explored their new home and played with all the animals. They were happy and peaceful in the lovely Garden of Eden.

Adam and Eve were busy in the garden. There was much to be done. They enjoyed being together and helping each other. The garden must have been a very warm place to live, because Adam and Eve didn't wear any clothes. They weren't embarrassed and ashamed because there was no sin. The world was pleasant and beautiful.

But there was something unlovely in God's world. That was Satan and his angel friends. Sometimes Satan is called the Devil. You may wonder how these sinful creatures got into God's world.

Before God made the world, He lived with His angels. All of God's angels served Him then, just like boys and girls of today should. But one of the angels God had made thought he could be as great and powerful as the One who made him. This can't be. It is a sin for anyone to think that he is as good or better than God. When this angel sinned, God had to send him away from heaven. This sinful angel was Satan, and he took other angel friends with him.

When God made the beautiful Garden of Eden, Satan came to visit it. He wanted others to sin and be like him. He thought and thought about how he would get Adam and Eve to disobey God.

A Wicked Trick

(Genesis 3:1–7)

At last Satan knew exactly what he would do to trick Adam and Eve. He would enter a snake and wait for a time when he could talk to one of them alone. It would be much easier to trick just one person, he thought.

One day he noticed the perfect moment. Eve was sitting by herself in the shade, waiting for the warm afternoon sun to go down. Suddenly she realized that she wasn't alone, because a voice asked, "Eve, did God tell you that you couldn't eat from all of the trees in the garden?"

"You're right," answered Eve. "We may eat from all of them except one. We may not eat from the Tree of Knowledge of Good and Evil. That's the tree right over there. It's in the middle of the garden." Eve pointed to it. Then she added, "God said that Adam and I would die if we ever eat any of the fruit from that tree."

Satan smiled. "So that's what God said. Oh, Eve! You won't die if you eat from it. In fact, if you do, you will be like God. You will know good from evil." Then Satan waited.

Eve glanced quickly at the tree. She walked over to it. She noticed how large and ripe the fruit was. How tasty it looked! While she stood there she thought to herself, "If I eat this fruit I'll be wise."

Then she forgot what God had said. She picked one of the nicest pieces and began to eat. She did exactly what God had told her not to do. She called to Adam and he ate some of it too. Both of them, Adam and Eve, ate from the tree which God had forbidden.

Satan was so very pleased. His wicked trick worked. Both Adam and Eve sinned.

Leaving Home

(Genesis 3:8–17, 23–24)

God knew what had happened to His world. He knew that Adam and Eve had disobeyed Him. So he looked for them in the garden. He called out, "Adam, Eve, where are you?"

Adam answered, "We're hiding. We are so ashamed because we disobeyed You. And we are naked. We tried to put some fig leaves together to cover ourselves." Adam and Eve crouched down behind the bushes. Then Adam added, "We're afraid."

God said, "Adam, how do you know you are naked? Why are you and Eve so embarrassed? Did you eat from the Tree of Knowledge of Good and Evil?"

Adam quickly said, "Well, it was really Eve's fault. She gave me a piece of the fruit, so I did take some."

Then God called to Eve, "What have you done? Did you eat the fruit from the tree?

Eve was ashamed because she knew that she had sinned. Her face turned red and she felt hot. But she knew that she had to answer God's question. She said, "It was really Satan's fault. He tricked me. He told me that I would be very wise if I ate, so I did take a piece."

Then God turned to the snake and said, "Because you did this, you will have to crawl around on your belly for the rest of your life. You will eat the dust from the ground."

Adam and Eve were frightened as they listened. Then God looked at Eve and said, "Because you have sinned, Eve, you will have pain when you have children. And your husband will rule over you." And to Adam He said, "You will have to work very hard. When it is hot you will sweat and your back will get tired. You will have to work this hard to make a living and have enough to eat, and some day you will die."

Before God left them, He made clothes

out of animal skins so Adam and Eve would have something to wear. What a sad day this was! Now God's peaceful and lovely world was covered with sin. God made Adam and Eve leave the beautiful Garden of Eden. To make sure that they didn't come back, He put angels and a flaming sword to guard the gate.

Hard Work

(Genesis 4:1–2)

Now the world was very different from when God created it. Adam and Eve worked so hard. Things were just like God said they would be. Adam planted a garden and he had to work to make it grow. Eve had to cook the food. She didn't have shiny pots and pans. She had no cans of food she could open, and she didn't have a dishwasher. Living was hard work.

The animals were different too. They chased and pounced to kill each other for food. Birds pecked and clawed. Eagles swooped to get their supper.

Before sin, Adam could tumble and play with the largest of all lions. But now he had to be very careful. A hungry lion or bear could kill him in a moment.

Diseases killed some of the plants and grasses. Or if the sun was too hot it would scorch the leaves. The burned plants would turn yellow and brown and then die. Sometimes insects ate the plants.

At times Adam and Eve got sick. Their stomachs ached or their feet were sore. If they felt too badly, they had to rest for a few days, like you do when you are ill.

Later two boys were born to Adam and Eve. Sometimes they played together and had fun. But other times they kicked and hollered and fought.

Yes, sin was in the world and it is still here today. God says, "For all have sinned and come short of the glory of God" (Romans 3:23).

44

The
Good News

God's Perfect Son
(John 3:16, 17)

God loves us very much, even though He doesn't love our sins. He wanted to save us so we could live with him forever. The only way would be for someone to take our place; someone perfect, without sin; someone willing to take our punishment for us.

God has a Son. He loves this Son a lot. This Son never sinned, not even once!

God thought about our sins and His perfect Son. God decided on a plan to save us. He would send His Son, His only Son, to this world to take our place. That Son would have to live on earth, die, and suffer the pain of living apart from God.

Just think about this plan for a little while. Oh, how God loved His Son, but He loved us too. God loved us so much that He was willing to send His Son down to earth to give us clean hearts. What a wonderful God we have! The next stories will tell you how this exciting plan worked.

Earthly Parents for Jesus
(Luke 1:26–31)

God's Son would live in this world just as we do. He would need feet, hands, head, arms . . . a body like ours. And so God sent Him to this world as a baby. God was His Father. But a lady named Mary would be His mother. This baby would still be God like His Father. But He would be a regular person too, like His mother. He would be God and man together.

An angel came to Mary and said, "You are going to have a baby, and you will call him Jesus. I know you aren't married, but don't worry. God is the Father of this baby. Jesus is His Son." Then the angel left Mary alone to think.

Mary was excited. She was thrilled. She would be the mother of God's Son, baby Jesus! She was eager to tell her boyfriend, Joseph, the good news. They were planning to get married. Joseph would want to know.

When Joseph learned that Mary was going to have a baby he was a little worried. They weren't married yet. What would people say?

But God spoke to Joseph too. One night while he was sleeping and dreaming, one of God's angels came into his dreams. The angel said, "Joseph, don't be afraid. Mary is going to have God's Son, Jesus. He will save His people from their sins. Go ahead, you and Mary should get married."

Joseph felt much better about it now. God's son, Jesus, would have an earthly father to care for Him.

Joseph did what the angel said and took Mary as his wife.

After they were man and wife, Joseph and Mary were eager for this child to be born. Jesus, the Savior of men, would grow up in their home!

Born in a Manger
(Luke 2:1–7)

About six months later the governor sent out a law ordering everyone to go back to the city where they were born. He wanted to count the people so he knew how much tax money he should collect. This happened very close to the time Mary's baby was ready to be born. Traveling now would be hard.

But it was a command. Everyone had to go. So Joseph packed a few things and put Mary on a donkey. She couldn't walk far because the baby was so large. She rode the donkey while Joseph led the way.

They traveled for a long time, days and nights. It was about seventy-five miles. That's a very long ride, especially on a donkey. Ask your dad or mom how far that is. Wouldn't that be a long trip?

When Mary and Joseph arrived in Bethlehem they looked for a room to sleep in. But everyone they asked had no extra room. So many people were in town that every bed was filled!

Mary was tired. Joseph's feet burned from the long walk. They would have to stay somewhere. Finally one man said that they could sleep on the hay in his barn. Joseph and Mary were glad. At least they could sleep!

While they rested on the hay, they heard some cattle chewing their feed. Others were sleeping noisily. There were the sounds and smells of animals. It certainly wasn't fancy, but it was a place to rest.

That night, on the hay in the barn, God's Son was born. Baby Jesus, the Savior of all men, was born in a barn. God must have loved us a lot to send His only Son to be born in a barn. Instead of having doctors and nurses around Him, Baby Jesus was surrounded by cattle!

Mary wrapped some clothes around Him and laid Him in a box that held cattle feed. Imagine! Baby Jesus didn't even have a baby bed of His own. He was laid in a manger. And that's how Jesus came to this earth.

(Luke 2:8–14)

While Jesus was being born in the barn, the people in the houses nearby didn't even know it. But outside the city there was a lot of excitement.

There were shepherds caring for their sheep. The stars stood watch over the snoozing lambs. The shepherds lay on the hillside dozing. Every once in a while one would awaken to check that the flock was safe. Then he would doze off again. The country was quiet and restful.

Suddenly the shepherds jerked to attention. They were startled by a brilliant light. It was an angel . . . a real one! They covered their faces

quickly.
Their sleep-
ing eyes
weren't
ready for
light, espe-
cially not
such a
dazzling one.

For a
moment they
shook with fear.
They were just plain scared.
Should they run? Should they try to hide?

As they wondered what to do, the angel said, "Please don't be afraid. I've got good news for everyone! This very night Jesus, the Savior, has been born. You'll find Him lying in a manger."

Just as the angel stopped talking it seemed as if God pulled back the dark night curtain. For out of the heavens came a choir of angels. They were singing. They were happy. They sang loud praises to God! The hillsides buzzed with the glory and excitement. Christ, the Savior, was born!

Eager Visitors

(Luke 2:15–20)

When the angels had finished their singing they went back into heaven. The dark night sky covered the earth again. The shepherds were anxious. They couldn't hurry fast enough to see this baby. A couple of them might have stayed to care for the sheep. But surely most of them rushed off to the city. They were going to see the Savior.

As they came near the city, they started looking in barns. And sure enough, after peeking into different ones, they found Joseph, Mary, and Jesus. It was true! It was all true! Here lay the baby Savior in a manger in front of their own eyes!

The shepherds talked excitedly. They told Joseph and Mary about what had happened on the hillside. Other people heard the chattering and came in to listen too. They talked about the angels, the singing, and what the angel messenger had said.

The good news of Jesus spread quickly. Many people came from around the city, hoping to see the Savior from sin. Such good news soon traveled throughout the whole town. Everybody heard about it.

People didn't have telephones and ra-
dios and televisions. But the news spread
almost as fast. People couldn't wait to tell
their neighbors and friends. This was
good news!

A Perfect Child

(Luke 2:39–40)

Jesus' mother and father stayed in
Bethlehem for a short time. Then they
hurried off to Egypt to hide from King

Herod who was looking for this new baby King. After a few years they finally headed for Nazareth, their hometown.

Back in Nazareth Joseph got back to his work quickly. He was a carpenter. He probably had a lot of tables, chairs, and cabinets to make. He had been out of town for a long time. He must have been behind in his orders for furniture.

Mary was busy too. She had a little boy to take care of. And you know how much work little children can be. Don't you think that Joseph and Mary had fun seeing Jesus crawl around? Then He learned how to walk and talk. I'm sure they were very happy parents.

But there was one thing about Jesus

that was different from that of any other child. He never sinned. He was perfect, remember? He is the Son of God!

He didn't talk back to his parents. He always did what they asked Him to do. He didn't cry and pout if He didn't get His way. He shared His toys. Yes, He was a perfect child.

Lost and Found

(Luke 2:41–50)

The Bible doesn't tell us very much about Jesus when He was a little boy. The next time we read about Him He is twelve years old.

Joseph and Mary went to Jerusalem with many of their friends and their children. They went to celebrate a holiday. It was another long trip. Walking goes quite slowly, especially with little ones along.

When the feast and the celebration were over, the whole group started their journey home. The children were gathered. Everything was packed. The donkeys were lined up. Slowly the line started moving . . . back to Nazareth.

Joseph and Mary thought that Jesus was with the group of children. They didn't bother to check on Him. After all, He was twelve years old now. He could get along pretty well by Himself.

When the group stopped for the night, they looked for Jesus. They asked the other boys and girls. They asked their friends. But no one had seen Him. Jesus was missing!

Joseph and Mary left the others quickly. They went back to Jerusalem. It took a day to walk back. They asked in the city market and at the stores. They asked people standing in the streets. They asked children playing in the road. But for three days they heard nothing about Him. Joseph and Mary were frantic!

On the fourth day they went to the Temple. As they walked up the steps, they thought they heard a familiar voice. It sounded like their son. Could it be?

Was He still alive? They went into the back of the Temple. Sure enough! There sat Jesus talking with the ministers and teachers. They were talking about grown-up things. It was important talk. The men were amazed at this twelve-year-old child!

Mary hurried to Jesus and scolded Him, "So, why did you do this to us? We've been worried about you. We have been looking all over town."

Jesus answered His mother. But He answered her in a strange way. He said, "Why did you look for me? Don't you know that I am here to do my Father's work?"

His parents didn't really understand. Jesus did go back home with them. And He stayed with them for many years. But Jesus was trying to help them understand that He was really God's Son. His Heavenly Father would always come first. His Father had a plan for Him . . . a plan to save sinners.

Acts
of Hate

The First Murder

(Genesis 4:1–12)

The Bible, God's Book, tells us about some people who listened to Satan. Others listened to God and obeyed Him. This chapter tells us about people who hated.

Adam and Eve had two sons named Cain and Abel. Cain was the older boy who grew up to be a farmer. How long he worked planting tiny seeds! When they were dry he had to carry water from the streams to the thirsty young plants. He spent many hours on his knees pulling out the tough weeds that tried to strangle the tender new shoots.

Abel chose to care for sheep. Every day he carefully led his flock to green, moist grass. As they nudged and nibbled their supper, Abel sang to them. But his eyes and ears were looking and listening for a hungry animal which might harm one of his little ones. They were very precious to him.

Satan worked very hard on these two young men. How often he came to them and urged them not to praise God. Sometimes he laughed at them. He stayed very close to them, hoping to keep God out of their hearts.

One day the two brothers brought offerings to God. Cain brought some of the fruit of his garden. Abel brought a young lamb, one of his fattest and best. Both of them put their offerings on the altar.

God looked down upon these offerings. But He also looked at the hearts of the young men who gave them. Abel's heart was thankful. He loved God. He had not listened to Satan. But Cain's heart did not love God. He had listened to Satan. When he brought his offering he wasn't even thinking of God and His goodness.

God said that He was very happy with Abel's offering because Abel's heart was loving. But God was angry with Cain for giving an offering when his heart wasn't even given with it. So God told Cain that He was very unhappy with him. He saw that Satan had entered his heart.

Cain was furious because his offering was not accepted. As he thought about it, he became jealous of his brother. Finally Cain began to hate Abel. Then Cain planned to do something very, very wrong. He waited for Abel in the field. And when he thought no one was looking, he killed his own brother, Abel. Then Cain hurried away, hoping no one saw him do it.

But God saw what Cain had done. He called to Cain asking, "Where is Abel, your brother?"

"I don't know," Cain called back. "Am I supposed to take care of him?"

God answered, "I saw what you did. Now I am going to punish you. You will have to spend the rest of your life running from place to place. But I will still care for you, Cain. I won't let anyone kill you as you have killed your brother." And on that day, Cain began his journey to a faraway country.

A Brother for Sale!

(Genesis 37:12–36)

A man named Jacob had many children. One of his children whom he liked very much was Joseph. He liked Joseph so much that he gave him a beautiful coat that was striped with many different colors.

Joseph's brothers began to hate him. They did this for two reasons. One was the lovely coat. It was more fancy than the coats Jacob had given them. And they became jealous because Joseph had many special dreams which meant that someday he would rule over all the brothers. Whenever Joseph told them about his dreams the brothers laughed and called him "The Dreamer." They hated him so much that they couldn't even talk nicely to him.

Father Jacob owned flocks of sheep. The older boys had to take these sheep far away where they could find tender grass. Sometimes the boys had to stay overnight because it was too far to come home. Whenever this happened Jacob worried about them.

One day when the brothers had been away for a little while, Jacob asked

Joseph, "Will you go and find your brothers for me? See how they are. Ask about the sheep. Then hurry home. I'm so anxious to hear about them." Joseph was happy to do these errands for his father. Before he left he put on his coat, the coat of many colors. Then he started out to find his brothers.

As Joseph came near the place where the brothers were, they noticed him coming. One laughingly said, "Hey, fellows! Here comes Dreamer Boy. I've got an idea. Let's kill him. All right?"

But the oldest brother said, "I don't think we should kill him. If you want to get rid of him, just throw him into that deep hole over there." All the brothers quickly agreed. And when Joseph got close to them, they ripped off his coat and put him in the pit before he could even ask them how they were.

Then the brothers sat down to eat. As they ate they talked about Joseph and what they should do with him. If they left him in the hole, he would surely starve to death.

Just as they were talking about this, they saw a group of men coming. They were rich men who bought and sold things. This would solve their problems. They would sell Joseph!

And they did exactly that. They sold him to be a servant boy. Soon Joseph was on his way to a strange, new country where he knew no one.

The brothers didn't dare to tell Father Jacob about their hating and selling Joseph. So they killed a lamb from their flock and put Joseph's beautiful coat in the blood. When they gave the bloody coat to Jacob they said, "See what we found? It was in the road. A wild animal must have killed Joseph." Not only did they hate, they also had lied to cover up their wicked deed.

A Jealous King

(1 Samuel 19:8–10)

King Saul was a jealous king. He was jealous of a young man in his kingdom. He disliked the lad because he could do so many things better than the King himself. He was an army officer who won many battles. He was a very good musician. And so many people in the kingdom learned to love him. Even King Saul's own children and servants loved this young man whose name was David.

When the King knew that the people in his kingdom loved David more than him, he became angry, so angry in fact, that he planned to kill David. How care-

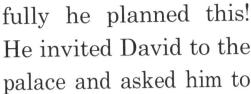

fully he planned this! He invited David to the palace and asked him to play a song for him on the harp. While David's fingers were running over the musical strings, King Saul pulled out his long hunting spear. He aimed carefully and quickly. Then in a moment he flung it straight toward David. King Saul was hoping to get rid of this young man forever.

But David was very alert. Out of the corner of his eye he had seen what the King was doing. He jumped off his stool just in time to save his life. Quickly David left the palace.

For many years David had to run from Saul because Saul's heart was so full of evil hatred for him. After Saul was an older man he asked David to forgive him for this sin. At last David no longer had to run from the hating heart of King Saul.

Tricked into a Lions' Den

(Daniel 6:1–24)

Daniel was a man whose heart was filled with love for God. He lived a good life and did his work very carefully. He was kind and loving toward those who worked for him. That is why most people liked him. King Darius liked him so very much that he decided to name Daniel as the most important man under himself. He called Daniel the First President.

Can you imagine what an important position this was? There were other men in the kingdom who wanted this job. When they heard that Daniel got the job instead of one of them, they became jealous. By now you know that when people get jealous they often do sinful things. And that is just what happened to these men.

One day they got together to make a plan against Daniel. He was such a godly man they knew it would be almost impossible to catch him doing something wrong. They also knew that Daniel prayed to God every day.

When their plan was carefully worked out they went to the King and said, "King Darius, live forever! You are such a good king that we have decided to make a law saying that everyone must worship you and only you for the next thirty days. And if anyone should be caught praying to another god, we will throw him immediately into the lions' den."

King Darius thought for a moment about this law. He could find nothing wrong with it, so he signed the paper and their wicked plan became a law. The men were thrilled! Have you figured out how their plan will work? Do they really like the King so much? Or are they trying to get rid of Daniel?

Even though Daniel heard about this law, he knew he could not pray to King Darius. Though Darius was a nice man and Daniel liked the King, he was not God. So Daniel opened his windows and prayed to the Lord God just as he always did, three times each day.

The plan had worked. Daniel's enemies saw him praying to God, and they hurried to the King. When the King heard what Daniel had done, he realized he had been tricked. He loved Daniel so. But the law could not be changed.

The guards were called to bring Daniel, and he was put into a den full of hungry, angry lions. A big stone was rolled in front of the den and the hole was sealed shut.

That night the King was so unhappy. One of his best men, his friend, was surely dead by now. All night long the King worried about Daniel. That's right. King Darius didn't sleep a wink!

That same night the men who had planned this trick were overjoyed. They were rid of Daniel at last! Now one of them could be made First President of the kingdom. They laughed to think of how easily their plan had worked.

When the King got up in the morning he hurried to the lions' den. He listened. He couldn't hear Daniel. Everything was deathly still. The King's heart saddened. But, just to be sure, he shouted, "Daniel, Oh, Daniel. Did your God save you?" King Darius really didn't expect an answer. He was sure that Daniel was dead.

But Daniel called out, "Oh, King Darius. My God sent an angel to close the mouth of every lion here. Not one of them has bitten me. I'm not even scratched!"

The King's mouth dropped open. He couldn't believe his own ears. Daniel, alive? He was so thrilled that he lost no time in calling men to pry the stone from the door of the den. And when the King looked in he saw Daniel sitting right in the middle of all the lions. They were lying around him like gentle, purring kittens. What a powerful God! Daniel was saved!

The men who hated Daniel and thought of this wicked plan were punished. King Darius threw them into the lions' den.

Stones for Love

(Acts 7:54–60)

The Bible tells about a missionary whose name was Stephen. He was a very busy man who loved God and worked hard for Him. Stephen preached to many people. He healed their sicknesses. He told them about Jesus so their hearts could become clean. Whenever he talked to people, some wanted a new heart and a new life.

But there were some men in the city where Stephen was preaching who did not love God. They didn't want others to love God either. Their hearts were given to Satan. So they waited for a chance to get Stephen into trouble.

They listened to him preach. They watched him. How eagerly they hoped to find something wrong. But they could find nothing. They would have to lie about things Stephen did. They sent men to tell the rulers that Stephen was making fun of God Himself! Now isn't that a strange lie to tell? Stephen loved the Lord. Would he laugh at the God he loved? Of course not! He would only speak the truth.

Because of this lie Stephen was

brought to the courtroom. The men repeated their lie and then Stephen was given a chance to answer them. But Stephen didn't even try because the lie seemed so foolish.

Instead Stephen began to preach to the rulers, the men who had lied, and to all others in the courtroom. Everyone listened closely. Stephen talked about God. He told the truth. The men who thought of the lies and the men who had told them became uncomfortable. The longer they listened the more angry they became. When they could stand it no longer they grabbed Stephen, even while he was standing and preaching. They dragged him out of the courtroom and down the streets of the city.

When they arrived outside the city they took off their coats. They wanted nothing to stop them or get in their way. They were determined to kill this man!

They looked for rocks, not little stones.

As quickly as they found them they threw them at Stephen. And while they threw stones at him, Stephen prayed: "Lord Jesus, receive my spirit." And then Stephen died. He was killed by people with hate in their hearts.

Deeds
of Love

A Traveling Friend

(Luke 10:30–37)

Hearts can hate, but hearts can also love. Some stories from the Bible tell about hearts that love God and men.

This story is one that Jesus told. It is about a man who was taking a trip. He was walking along the road on his way to Jericho. Just as he turned a corner, robbers jumped out from behind and pounced on him. They grabbed his wallet, ripped his clothes, and left him in the road alone. He was bleeding badly and needed care quickly.

Soon a priest came down the same road. A priest is the head of a church, a minister. When he saw the wounded man he quickly crossed the street so he wouldn't have to look at his beaten body. Surely the heart of this priest did not love.

Then a Levite came. He noticed something lying in the road. Why, it looked like a man's body! When he realized that it was a person, he quickly crossed the street, just as the priest had done. Can you imagine that? A priest, the head of the church, didn't help and a Levite, the priest's helper, didn't help either. They talked about love in their churches but their hearts did not love.

Then a man from Samaria came by on his donkey. He is called the Samaritan. He glanced ahead. "A man lying in the middle of the road?" he asked himself. When he reached the man he saw how badly he was wounded. Quickly and tenderly he poured wine and soothing oils on his bleeding sores, wrapped the cuts and bruises. Carefully he lifted the man onto his donkey and walked into the next city.

When they arrived the Samaritan looked for an inn. He left the donkey at the animals' stall and carefully carried the wounded man to a room. This man needed so much rest and care. Again he checked all the sores to be doubly sure he would be all right for the night. Soon both men were fast asleep.

In the morning the Samaritan paid for the rooms. To the inn manager he said, "Please take very good care of this man. I know it'll cost a lot of money. But I will surely pay you the next time I come to your city."

How can you tell which man in this story had a heart full of love? He even loved a stranger. That is why this man is called the "Good Samaritan."

Ninety-Nine Plus One

(Luke 15:1–7)

Jesus tells us many stories in the Bible. Another one about love is called "The Good Shepherd." This shepherd had exactly one hundred sheep. He knew them just as well as mothers know their children. By looking at the way they held their ears and tails, the spots on their bodies, their eyes, or the way they walked, he knew just which one was which. The sheep, too, could tell the shepherd's voice from others.

You know how mothers tuck their little ones in at night. This shepherd did the same with his sheep. As he let them under the gate and into the fold, he counted each one to be certain all came back with him at night.

And every night when the last sheep was in, he had reached one hundred. Then the shepherd himself could lie down and sleep peacefully because all of his flock were safely home.

But one evening he had reached only ninety-nine when the last sheep was counted. His heart pounded and he got a lump in his throat. "Oh, no! One of my sheep is missing!" his heart cried. And he counted them again, so carefully. But again he counted only ninety-nine.

It took only a moment for him to decide that he must look for the little lamb. He knew exactly which one was the missing sheep. Quickly he left the fold.

He climbed the rolling hills and walked through scratching briar patches. He slipped on rocks that led down to deep ditches. As he walked he called to his lost sheep. Then he stopped so he could listen in complete silence. But no answer came. Then he would walk a little farther and call again, hoping for an answer.

The shepherd in this story is called the "Good Shepherd." He was good because he didn't stop looking even though he knew that he still had ninety-nine back in the fold. The hills were rocky and dangerous but he kept wandering, searching, and calling. Finally he heard a faint, Baa-a-a. He stopped and listened for the direction of that tired sheep cry. Quickly he started toward the sound.

When he found his little sheep he carefully put the frightened lamb in his arms and started for the fold. At last the lost was found! The shepherd was weak and his bones ached from climbing and walking in the darkness of the night. But his flock would be together again—all one hundred of them.

Sometimes Jesus is called the Good Shepherd too. He loves every girl and boy so much that he is willing to look for them and give them clean, loving hearts.

Perfume for Jesus

(John 12:1–8)

Mary loved Jesus so much. She became so excited whenever He was coming to visit and stay for supper. For this evening she had gotten something very special because she wanted to show Jesus that she really loved Him. It was very expensive perfume. It cost so much that Mary must have saved a long time for it.

While all the guests were at the supper table, Mary got the costly perfume and poured it, all of it, over Jesus' feet. Then she wiped His feet with her hair. Just think, Mary was willing to spend that much money just to wipe the feet of her friend, Jesus.

No sooner had she done this then Judas, one of the guests who loved money, jumped to his feet and shouted, "Mary, how stupid of you! That perfume could have been sold for $48. At least you could have given the money to the poor!"

But Jesus said, "Quiet, Judas. Leave Mary alone. She has done this because she loves me."

Acts of
Unbelief

A Special Promise

Abraham and Sarah leaned back in their outdoor chairs. They were getting old and they often sat outside in front of their tent house and watched the children who tussled and tumbled around their yard. Maybe the reason they liked to see little ones so much was because they had no children of their own.

Hundreds of cattle and sheep grazed and wandered on the many acres of land Abraham owned. He and Sarah were very rich and could buy most anything they wanted. But they couldn't buy a child. Besides, they were old and gray now. They knew that God doesn't usually give tiny babies to older people. So they tried to forget how much they wanted a baby of their very own.

Late in the afternoon of a scorching day Abraham saw some men coming to his tent. They looked like visitors so he ran out to say hello. He gave them water to wash their dusty, tired feet and invited them to sit in the shade of a large, leafy tree.

Perhaps you serve a cold drink or tea or coffee to guests that stop in for a chat. But Abraham told Sarah to prepare a feast... fresh cakes, tender young beef, creamy butter, and cool milk. Abraham knew that these were special men. They were messengers of God!

While the guests and Abraham ate this tasty food, the messengers told him something quite surprising. They said, "Abraham, your wife is going to have a baby boy."

Sarah stood just inside the tent. She happened to hear what the men had said. Before she could think, she laughed and thought, "Me? Have a baby? Can't be! I'm too old!"

You may be surprised to learn that Sarah loved God. But Satan kept working in her heart. He tried to get Sarah to think that God couldn't do hard jobs like giving a baby to an older lady. Satan's plan worked. Sarah laughed. She thought that God surely couldn't do this!

But God showed Sarah that He meant

just what He had said. When it was exactly time, Sarah had a baby ... and it was a boy! Abraham and Sarah named him Isaac. They were so very happy to have a son. How sorry Sarah must have been that she had laughed about God's promise.

Complaining People
(Numbers 20:1–11)

The Israelites were God's special people. He chose them to be His own and He cared for them. One time God led them into the desert to live. While they were living there, they lived in tents.

Tent living in the desert can be quite uncomfortable, you know. They had to eat whatever food they could find, perhaps only wild berries. They cooked in large pots over an open fire. If it rained the ground was muddy and slippery. If they had no rain for many days it became very hot and stuffy. Drinking water was hard to find.

You may wonder why God would take His chosen people to such a place. He did it because He was leading His people to a new and beautiful place to live. They had to travel by foot to get there. There were no airplanes or trains in those days.

And so they traveled step by step by step. Once they couldn't find water where they stopped to camp. Another time they could find no food, no wild berries, absolutely nothing! The people went to their leader and nagged and cried, "Why, O why, did God ever bring us to this place?" You see, they weren't trusting God. They thought that God wouldn't take care of them.

Maybe you're thinking that you would complain too. "After all," you say, "if I was hungry, thirsty, dusty, and my feet were sore from walking, I think I'd complain a little too."

Just in case you're thinking that, think about how the Israelites lived before God led them away.

It was in a land where they were made slaves. It was a hot country where people made buildings from mud bricks. The Israelites had to make these bricks, one by one. If they didn't work fast enough, the Egyptians beat them to make them hustle a bit faster. When they did work just as fast as they possibly could, the work masters expected them to make even more bricks the next time. Sometimes they worked and sweated under the broiling sun until they fainted! But the king of the land didn't feel sorry for them. They had to keep making bricks.

Yet there had been something even worse than being treated so badly by their masters. That was the time the king of the land sent his messengers to every Israelite house to check for baby boys. The king was very cruel and didn't want any Israelite baby boys to live. It broke the fathers' and mothers' hearts to watch the messengers take away their precious baby boys.

Now do you understand why the Israelites had no reason to complain? God had taken them out of that land of miserable slavery. Living in the desert surely wasn't the most pleasant place, but think how much better it was than being beaten and killed!

The Israelites had no reason to believe that God wouldn't care for them, did they? When there was no water, God opened a rock and out bubbled fresh, clean water. When they were hungry God sent bread from heaven. God did take care of His people.

A Man Who Couldn't Talk

(Luke 1:11–22, 57–64)

Have you ever met anyone who couldn't talk? Someone besides a little baby? That is exactly the problem that

Zacharias, a priest in the Temple, had. Oh, yes, he could twist his tongue. His jaw moved easily when he ate. And even his lips moved. But whenever he wanted to speak, not a sound would come . . . not even a squeak or a whisper!

Zacharias wasn't born with this problem. He was an old man and he had had this only a short time. He couldn't speak because God had punished him.

Zacharias and his wife, Elizabeth, were old and had no children—just like Abraham and Sarah. An angel of God came before him and said, "Your wife is going to have a little boy. And when he is born, you shall name him John. He will grow up to love God and will help do the Lord's work."

Zacharias was shocked at what he heard. He looked at the angel and questioned, "How can I be sure that this will really happen? You know that Elizabeth and I are very old."

God was disappointed in this man. He didn't believe God just as Sarah had not.

So God punished him by not allowing him to speak until after the baby was born. Wherever Zacharias went he carried writing materials with him. If someone asked him a question, he wrote the answer. What a bother that must have been! Can you imagine writing down every single word that you say in a whole day? at the table? at school? a ball game? What a chore!

When Elizabeth's baby was born, Zacharias couldn't speak right away. He still carried his materials with him. It was when the baby was eight days old that God gave his voice back to him.

Zacharias and Elizabeth took the baby to the Temple to promise his life to God. The relatives and friends were there with them. When it was time to name the baby, everyone said that his name should be Zacharias, like his father.

But Elizabeth immediately said, "No, we are going to name him John."

"John?" everyone asked, quite surprised. "Nobody in your whole family is named John." They looked at Zacharias as if to say, "Do you want him to be named John?"

Zacharias quickly wrote, "His name will be John."

The very second he wrote this God gave him back his voice. Zacharias told all the people how good God was for giving them this little boy even when they were very old.

Deeds
of Faith

(Exodus 2:1–10)

"A baby boy," the family whispered. They looked at each other in quick, nervous glances. Each one was thinking, "Where can we hide him? How can we keep him from crying? Hurry, or the king's messengers will hear!"

"That's strange," you say. "Why hide the baby? Is there something wrong with it? When a baby is born in our family we can't wait to tell our friends and relatives. Why are these people so worried? Why don't they want the king's messengers to hear the baby crying?"

This little baby boy was Moses. He was born to an Israelite family who loved and trusted God. But the king of their land was wicked. He made a law that all Israelite boy babies must be thrown into the river. Naturally they didn't want to drown their baby. So they hid him.

Hiding a baby isn't easy, especially when it cries so long and loud. You know how noisy little babies can be. That's why the family kept all their windows and doors closed. They hurried to rock or feed him whenever he cried. And it worked . . . at least for three months.

Now the baby was so big that they couldn't hide him any longer. Mother had to think of another way. She prayed and asked God to help her find a way to keep her little baby boy alive. She trusted God and God gave her an idea.

She walked by the river for a special reason. She was looking for the long reeds that grow there. She picked enough, then hurried home where she weaved a little basket. She covered it with mud and with tar so it wouldn't leak. It was very important that this little basket didn't leak, because she was going to float her baby in the river. When the basket was ready she tenderly put the baby in it.

Sneaking the basket to the river was a difficult job. Each member of the family walked back and forth to the river making sure there were no guards near. When the path seemed safe, Mother quickly carried her precious baby to the river and put him in the weeds that grew near the edge. The younger sister, Miriam, stayed nearby. She pretended to be playing, but all the while she kept her eye on the little basket in which her little brother was lying.

Later that day the king's daughter came to the river for her daily bath. She waded into the water, enjoying its coolness. She noticed the unusual little basket and sent one of her maidens to get it. Curiously she looked in to find the Israelite baby boy. As soon as she saw him, she loved him.

Miriam, who was really watching that little basket every second, ran to the water's edge and called to the princess, "Would you like me to find a lady to take care of your little boy?"

The princess called back, "I certainly would! Will you find someone for me?"

Miriam hardly waited for her to answer. She jumped over the weeds and ran straight to her mother. When she got home she was so out of breath she could hardly tell the good news.

When Miriam's mother heard what had happened, she thanked God for helping her. Now she would be able to take care of her own baby boy, even though he now belonged to the princess. She could let him play outside, tumble, scream, and somersault. The guards wouldn't dare harm the son of the princess!

Five Stones and a Giant

(1 Samuel 17:4–11, 38–51)

The Israelites were in the middle of a battle. And they were worried. Their enemy had an excellent soldier. He was a giant whose name was Goliath. Every morning and evening he came to the edge of the battle line and shouted, "What's the matter? Are you guys afraid of me? Send someone over to fight me. If he can kill me, we'll be your slaves. But if I kill him, you'll be our slaves."

Whenever Goliath roared like this the Israelites worried all the more. Those men who went to see Goliath turned around and ran. He was huge! He stood about nine and one-half feet tall. Who, just who, could they find who would dare to fight this monstrous man?

While they were discussing this problem, a little brother of several of the soldiers came with food from their father. This young boy was David. He listened to their worried voices. He had also heard the giant's teasing.

He boldly said, "I'm not afraid of that giant. I am on God's side. He'll take care of me and help me. I'll get out my slingshot and look for just the right stones." Off he ran, looking.

The soldiers worried about David. He was so young and so small. They didn't trust God to take care of little David. But David was so determined, they let him go to meet Goliath.

As David walked toward the giant everyone on both sides held their breath. There was a deathly silence ... until the giant laughed out loud. He teased and hollered, "What do you think I am? A dog? All you have is a little stick to fight with." Goliath's angry words echoed across the valley.

But David's knees didn't even shake. He shouted right back. "Maybe you do have a hunting spear and a lot of other weapons; but I've got God with me and God will help me kill you." While David talked he kept walking toward the giant. He was not afraid.

When the moment was right, David took out his slingshot, put a stone in it, and whirled it around. In an instant a smooth little stone went whirring through the air. It hit Goliath right in the head and he fell crashing and clanging to the ground. Goliath was dead. David put his trust in God and God helped him.

Three in a Fire

(Daniel 3)

The musical instruments sounded. The music could be heard for miles. People rushed out of their homes and fell on their knees to worship the king's image. It was massive! The golden idol stood about ninety-five feet high and was nine feet wide. Can you imagine how big that is?

The king had ordered everyone who could hear the music to fall on their knees and worship this idol. Anyone who refused would be thrown into a furnace of fire. The king had sent the message to everyone. And almost everyone obeyed.

One day messengers of the king arrived to report, "Oh, king! There are three men who will not worship your new image. They just refuse to do it!"

The king flew into a rage and demanded, "Bring those men to me immediately."

In a short time the messengers returned with the three men: Shadrach, Meshach, and Abednego. They were brought before the king, who shouted, "Is it true that you do not worship my golden image?" As he spoke his face grew purple-red with anger.

"It's true, O king," the three men answered. "Our God lives in heaven. We trust Him to save us from the furnace of fire. And He can save us from you. We cannot worship your golden image. We will worship only the true God."

The king was furious! How would any-one dare to disobey him? He would punish them. And he would do it quickly. The king decided to show the people that no one could disobey him! The king shrieked, "Heat the furnace hotter and throw these men in!"

Shadrach, Meshach, and Abednego

were tied tightly and thrown into the middle of the furnace.

The men who had thrown them in were trapped by the heat and the flames. They fainted and fell to the ground. In a minute they were dead.

And Shadrach, Meshach, and Abednego? How were they? They could hardly be seen through the thick and wiggling smoke. But the king came to look. He strained his eyes in disbelief. What? Four men? Frantically he called to the guards. "Didn't we throw three men into the fire? Weren't they bound with ropes? I see four men ... and they're walking around! One man looks almost ... almost like the Son of God! Guards! Guards! Hurry! Look! Do you see what I see?"

The king and his men rushed near the fire. The king called, "Shadrach, Meshach, Abednego! Come out of the fire!"

The three men walked out of the fire and toward the king. Their hair wasn't touched! Their clothes weren't black and ragged. And even more amazing, they didn't even smell like smoke!

When the king saw them, he turned toward the astonished people and spoke, "The God of Shadrach, Meshach, and Abednego is a powerful God. He sent His angel to care for these men. Never, no never, say a word against their God. For no other God can do such miracles!"

Just a Touch
(Mark 5:25–34)

She listened hopefully to her friend who told her about a man named Jesus. He had been healing so many people, some who couldn't walk, some who were blind, and He had even brought a dead man back to life. "Can it be true?" she excitedly asked her friend. "These are miracles indeed. When will He come to our town? If I only could see Him, I know He would make me well!"

For twelve years this woman had had a bleeding disease. She had traveled many miles and seen many doctors. But none could heal her. All her money was gone and now she was even feeling worse. She had to see Jesus! She believed that He could help her.

When she heard that Jesus was visiting the city, she got up very early in the morning to be certain not to miss Him. "This could be the most important day of my life," she thought to herself. Though she was weak from bleeding, she left her home and hurried toward town.

As she entered the streets of the city she saw crowds of people pushing and shoving. Jesus just had to be somewhere in the middle of all those people. She walked to the edge of the crowd and began slowly pushing her way toward Jesus.

The closer she came to Him, the harder it was to move. People were pushed so tightly together. It was impossible to budge them. Each one seemed like a solid, immovable pole. She dropped to her knees hoping that she could touch His clothes. Even that would help her to be healed of her bleeding.

Stretching her arm just as far as she could, she touched the very bottom of His coat. At the same moment she felt the blood stop flowing. But before she could even get up she heard Jesus ask, "Who touched me?"

Jesus' friends answered with disgust, "How can you tell who touched you? There are so many people pushing against you that it would be impossible to say."

"Oh, no" Jesus said, looking around. "Someone touched my clothes. I could feel healing power go out of my body."

Frightened, the woman confessed, "Lord, I touched you. I wanted to be rid of this bleeding. I just knew you could heal me." Smiling down at her, Jesus said, "Go home and be happy. Because you trusted me I've healed your body. And I've given you a clean heart."

A Big Surprise for a Little Man

(Luke 19:1–10)

Zacchaeus sat with his head in his hands. He was thinking about a problem he had. Today was the day that Jesus was coming to town. Wherever Jesus went there were such large crowds that it was very hard to push through to see Him. And, to make things even worse, Zacchaeus was a very little man. He was almost like some of the little people you may have seen.

As he sat there thinking, he got a brainstorm. "That's it," he shouted as he jumped up. "That's exactly what I'll do! I'll climb a tree."

He began looking for the perfect one. Not just any tree would do. At last he found a sycamore tree that seemed just right. It was next to the road that Jesus would use. He scrambled up to the biggest branch that leaned over the road. He wiggled around until he felt comfortable. Then he waited.

In a short time he heard voices from a

distance. He peeked through the leaves and looked. Sure enough! He could see the huge crowd. They were coming straight down the road, right toward him. Zacchaeus was so excited. He watched them come closer and closer. Soon he could see Jesus Himself.

Just as Jesus came to the tree, He looked right at Zacchaeus and said, "Zacchaeus, hurry, come down from that tree. I'm coming to your house for supper."

Zacchaeus couldn't believe what he heard. He was so surprised that he almost lost his balance. As fast as he could, he tumbled down and took Jesus to his home.

As they ate supper Jesus told Zacchaeus that if he believed that Jesus would clean his heart from sin he would go to heaven someday. Zacchaeus answered, "I do believe. I do. I do."

Jesus said, "Zacchaeus, today you became a child of mine because you have trusted me. I love you and will take care of you forever."

Acts of
Disobedience

A Statue of Salt

(Genesis 19:12–17, 26)

God's Book tells us about people who didn't do what He had told them. They sinned just as you and I do when we don't obey our parents, teachers, ministers, policemen, or others who care for us. Not obeying is called disobedience.

There were two cities, Sodom and Gomorrah, which were very wicked. The people sinned so greatly that God decided to destroy them completely...their homes, stores, animals, and crops. Everything had to be burned! Fire would come down from heaven and destroy the cities.

But there was one man named Lot whom God didn't want to destroy. He was married and had two daughters living at home. So the Lord sent two heavenly visitors to see him and warn his family about the coming danger.

When the visitors arrived in the city they were teased and mocked. They stayed inside Lot's house because the sinful men of the city wanted to get them. God's messengers weren't even safe in these two towns!

In the morning God's men told Lot, "Take your wife and daughters and run for your lives. Go as far away as those mountains over there and don't turn to look back, not even once. God is going to burn these cities to the ground."

Lot quickly answered, "Gentlemen, I'm afraid to stay in the mountains. We may starve or wild animals may kill us. May we go instead to that little city?" He pointed to a small city at the foot of a large mountain.

God's messengers said, "All right. You may go to that city, but hurry! Go quickly!"

Lot, his wife, and daughters began running. And God began to burn the cities. He sent fire pell-melling out of heaven like hail. Everywhere and on everything sizzling fire bombed.

Lot and his family could hear the noises of burning as they ran. People screamed, homes went up in smoke, trees snapped, buildings crackled as they fell, dying cattle cried out. But Lot's family ran on because God had said not to look back.

Lot's wife thought about everything she left behind, her home, nice clothes, and the city she loved. All of it would soon be ashes and soot. These thoughts kept pestering her until she turned her head just a little to take one last, short peek at her hometown. Just as she did, God turned her into a solid statue of pure white salt!

Lot and his daughters could hear that she was no longer with them. She didn't answer their calls. Her footsteps were silent. "What happened to her?" they asked each other as they ran. No one knew and no one dared to turn and look because of God's command.

Trouble for Pharaoh

(Exodus 7:10–25; 8:5–32)

Moses and Aaron stood in front of King Pharaoh and announced, "Our God, the God of the Israelites, commands you to let His people leave your land. You must let them go!"

But Pharaoh was stubborn. He shouted back, "I won't let them go." You see, the Israelites were his slaves. They did all the hard work in his kingdom. If he let all these people go, who would do the work? And so he said, "No!"

Because King Pharaoh disobeyed God, God told Moses to have Aaron stretch his walking stick over the waters of the kingdom. When he did this, every drop of water in every bowl, pond, lake, and river turned into red blood.

Fish can't swim and live in blood, you know. They turned over on their sides and died. Their bodies floated to the edge of the water and the beaches were soon covered with dead and rotting, stinking fish.

What happened when the people wanted to take a drink, take a bath, cook food, wash dishes, or water their gardens? Everywhere the water had turned to blood—right to the last drop.

For a long time the people of Pharaoh's kingdom were bothered by blood. Moses thought that Pharaoh would surely let the people leave now. And so he asked again. But Pharaoh shouted, "No! I will not, I will not!"

God told Moses to have Aaron stretch his stick over the river again. This time frogs came leaping and scrambling out. Not just a few came, but they kept coming out until frogs were everywhere; in the beds, cooking pots, dishes, food, washtubs, and the pockets of the people's clothes. Croaking and squiggling they came.

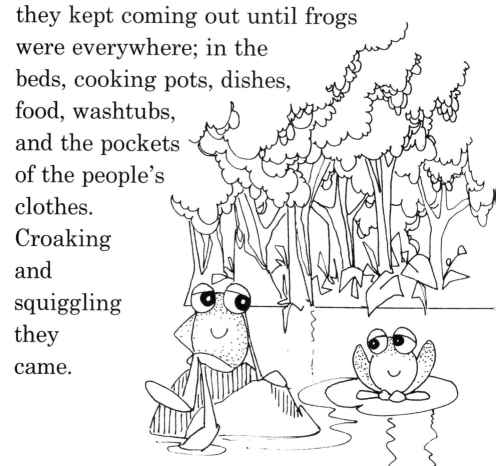

Pharaoh was so disturbed by them that he came to Moses saying, "Please, oh, please, take away these frogs and I will let the people go! If only we can get rid of all these frogs!"

God made all the frogs die. Now there were dead frogs everywhere. The people gathered them into huge piles . . . piles of stinking and spoiling frogs.

But when the frogs were gone, Pharaoh changed his mind. For punishment God had Aaron stretch his stick over the dust and tiny crawling lice appeared on all people and cattle. They lived in the hair of men and animals and bit their skin. People kept scratching their heads to get rid of the pests. They scratched until their heads were sore and bleeding, but the lice couldn't be killed.

Even that didn't make Pharaoh obey! So God sent swarms of flies to bother everyone, except the Israelites, God's people. This time only Pharaoh and his people were pestered. Flies buzzed in their ears and around their eyes. They landed on their noses and lips. The people almost went crazy trying to chase them away, but they couldn't get rid of them.

Pharaoh changed his mind again, but his heart was still just as hard as stone. He wouldn't let God's people leave after all of these awful plagues.

More Trouble
(Exodus 9, 10)

Then God sent a disease to all of the cattle of Pharaoh's land. It was a severe disease and all the cattle died: old and young, weak and strong, fat and thin. They fell over dead.

Still Pharaoh's heart was angry. His people begged and begged him to let the

Israelites go. They wanted to live in peace and pleasure again. But their stubborn King just wouldn't listen to their cries.

Next God sent boils to all the men and beasts. Boils are large red sores which are hard but terribly tender. These sores covered their whole bodies. They couldn't even lie down or sit without having great pain from the boils.

Another plague that God sent was hail, large round pieces of solid ice. Every garden and field was shredded to the ground. Their homes were shattered and pounded. Lightning flickered and thunder crashed.

Then God sent grasshoppers which covered the earth. They ate everything as they went. They mowed and shaved the earth. Finally only bare brown dirt could be seen across the land.

Darkness followed the grasshoppers. It was blacker than midnight for three days. The moon and stars didn't glitter, not even a little. People, animals, and pets stumbled through the days and nights. No one knew what time it was. They didn't know when to go to bed or get up. They bumped into things as they walked. Confusion was everywhere!

But Pharaoh still said, No! After all these dreadful things God sent to punish him, he still refused. God became angry with him. He planned to show Pharaoh that He meant what He said.

Trouble and Tears

(Exodus 12:21–36)

Moses told the Israelites about God's plan. He told them to pack and be ready to leave Pharaoh's land. He also told them to paint the top of their doors with the blood of a lamb. This would be a sign to keep them from receiving the next punishment God would send.

Night crept quietly into the kingdom. Israelites were preparing to leave, but Pharaoh and his people fell asleep easily, thinking that God had at last stopped bothering them. Yet that very night God sent an angel of death to every house except those that were painted with blood. The death angel gently touched the oldest child in every single home. Not a sound was made, but death had struck.

During the same night the king and his servants awoke. But in each house of Pharaoh's people, the oldest child didn't. Something was terribly wrong. Can you imagine how brokenhearted these people were when they realized what had happened?

Pharaoh, too, cried when he saw that his own precious child was no longer living. This touched and softened his hard, hard heart. At last he called for Moses, "Please, please, take the Israelites and

leave this land. Quickly
go before something
else happens to us!

When God gave
the command the
Israelites began to
move from Pharaoh's
land. Slowly they
inched out of the
country of slavery.
They were free at last! Joyfully the thousands of Israelites began their journey.

Dry Road Through the Sea

(Exodus 14:5–31)

Within a couple of days God's people
were stopped by the Red Sea. Moses asked
God to help them cross over. God helped
them that very night. He sent a strong
wind to push back the waters of the sea
until they stood up like cemented stone

walls. And the people began to walk across on the dry sea floor.

Two days also gave Pharaoh time to think. The longer he thought about losing all of his slaves, the more angry and impatient he became. When he could stand it no more, he called together his army and followed after the Israelites, hoping to catch them.

Pharaoh and his men caught up to them just as the last Israelites were walking across the dry sea floor. They hurried right into the sea after them. When the last Israelite climbed onto the shore, God hurled the walls of water back into the middle of the sea. Pharaoh and his men were covered with tons of water!

God punished Pharoah in a powerful way! What a sight! Pieces of chariots washed up on the beaches. Bits of broken wheels bobbed on the waves. Heavy weapons sunk to the bottom and began rusting. All of this was Pharaoh's punishment for disobedience!

Moses' Mistake

(Numbers 20:1–12)

Traveling through the desert was long and difficult. People complained to Moses about all the little things that they didn't like. One particular time they discovered that there was no water where they had camped. How disgusted they became. Whining and grumbling they came to Moses, "Whatever will we do now? There's not a drop of water near this place. The animals are thirsty and the children are hot and dusty. There's no water at all, not even for cooking. Things really cannot get much worse! If we have no water, we will surely die."

Moses cried to God, "See, Lord, how the people complain? They are really angry this time. Please help me give water to them."

God told Moses to go to a certain rock and speak to it. He promised that fresh water would gurgle and burst out of it. Then there would be water for everyone.

Moses listened to God. He too was worn from traveling. He was hot and his feet ached. He was tired of listening to the complaining Israelites.

When he walked to the rock, he was angry with them. Instead of speaking to the rock as God had told him, he furiously struck it with his cane, not once, but twice!

Water spurted out and hurried down the side of the rock.

The people grabbed pots and jugs. Quickly they filled them and scurried off to take care of their many chores. Now they were happy again, at least for a little while.

But God wasn't pleased, especially not with Moses. He had disobeyed. Instead of speaking to the rock, he hit it in a fit of temper.

Tenderly but firmly God spoke to Moses, "You have been a good leader of my people. You are bringing them nearer to the wonderful land I'm going to give them. But because you disobeyed, you'll not be allowed to go into that beautiful country. You may see it from a mountain-top, but you may not enter."

Moses was God's child and he loved God. But even God's children disobey. God had to punish Moses for this sin just as He will punish us for disobeying.

Man Overboard!
(Jonah 1, 2, 3:1–3)

God's voice visited Jonah one afternoon and gave him a command, "Go to Nineveh, Jonah! Preach the gospel to the people. They're so sinful. Tell them that their city will be overthrown if they don't ask for forgiveness." Quietly God slipped away, leaving Jonah alone to think about the command he had received.

But Jonah didn't want to preach. He ran away to a different city and got on a ship. He snuggled down into a corner and smiled and relaxed. He was so sure that he'd hidden from God.

How silly of him! Hide from God? It can't be done! God saw him sleeping peacefully in the ship. He sent a strong wind that stormed over the water. The boat slipped from tip to tip and edge to edge. Waves slammed against the sides like giant hammers. The captain called to the people to pray to their gods for safety. But Jonah slept on.

When the captain saw him napping, he shook him awake saying, "Get up, man! How can you sleep in a storm like this? Pray to your god for mercy!"

The other passengers were worried. They wondered whose fault this trouble could be. When they discovered that Jonah was the man, they begged, "Jonah, what shall we do? It is your fault that we are having this storm."

Jonah answered, "I guess you'll have to toss me overboard. Then the Lord will quiet the sea."

They did exactly that. Jonah was thrown over the side of the ship. Before he could drown, God sent a large sea creature to swallow him. Slowly he traveled down to its stomach. Can you think what it would be like to live inside the stomach of a fish? It must have been a whopper to take such a man-sized supper!

While Jonah lived inside this fish he prayed to God. He asked God to forgive him for disobeying and promised to go to Nineveh if God would save him and give him a second chance. Then Jonah waited as he rode inside this swimming fish.

Gliding through the water, the fish headed toward shore. Its stomach ached. Its supper wasn't as good as it seemed at first and this fish wanted to get rid of it fast. When it was as close to shore as a big fish can come, it opened its gigantic mouth and vomited. Jonah was coughed out and he tumbled onto shore. He rinsed himself off and waded back to the sand.

The next time God asked him to go to Nineveh, he was ready to go and obeyed.

Deeds of
Obedience

Pack Everything—We're Moving!

(Genesis 12:1–5; 13:14–18)

How do you think you would feel if God told you to move! Even if you knew exactly where you were going it would still be hard, wouldn't it? You'd have to leave your best friends, your favorite house and room, your school chums, and your church. Yes, you'd have to start all over in a new strange place.

That's just what God told Abram to do. He said, "Take everything you own and go to a new land. You don't even know where it is, but don't worry, for I will show you the way."

Abram and Sarai, his wife, began packing . . . dishes, furniture, tent houses, and clothes. Lot and his family did the same because they were going along. All of Abram's servants prepared to leave. Then there were Abram's many flocks and herds. They had to be gathered together. Picture in your mind what a long line that must have been!

If you were moving, you'd rent a truck or call a moving van. You could make a long journey in a few days. But all Abram had to use were wooden carts, horses, and donkeys. It took weeks and maybe even months!

Slowly the journey started. Animals clopped along. Saddles squeaked. Wagons and carts creaked as their wheels went round and round. Every night the noise quieted when the whole group stopped to camp and rest for the night.

Each day Abram started the journey again, wondering, "Where will God take me? What will the land be like? Will there be neighbors? I hope there's fresh water nearby. And I hope Sarai likes our new place!"

Each day they came closer to their new land. Each day Abram wondered if today would be the day they would arrive. He was anxious to see the new pastures and find the right spot to set up their home. It was like an exciting mystery.

Finally Abram and Lot separated. Their cattlemen were arguing and causing a lot of trouble. Lot and Abram decided that it would be best if they parted. Lot chose the land he wanted and headed in that direction with his family.

Then God called Abram and said, "Look to the south, north, east, and west of you. See the rolling land? I'm going to give you all of it, every inch you can see."

Abram stretched to take a closer look. He saw valleys and hills, pastures and fields. All of it, his! He was thankful to God for bringing him to this new home.

Bread for Tomorrow
1 Kings 17:8–17

Elijah was God's prophet. He spoke God's words to the people. And God took care of him. Sometimes God sent birds to bring him meat and bread. Elijah drank fresh, cool water from a brook. And when the brook dried up, the Lord sent him to another city. The Lord told him that a woman there would take care of him.

Elijah started out. He knew that somewhere in that city was a special person. God said so.

When Elijah walked into town, he saw a woman picking up sticks. She didn't look like she was very special. In fact, she looked like most other women. But Elijah was thirsty, so he spoke. "Hello, ma'am. Would you have time to get me a cup of water?"

"I'd be happy to," she said. "I'll be back in just a minute."

Elijah called out, "How about bringing me a slice of bread too?"

The woman's smile disappeared. She stopped and turned toward Elijah. "I'm so sorry. I can't give you a slice of bread. I don't have one. All I have is a little bit of flour. Not more than a cup. I have just a wee bit of oil. I was picking up sticks to build a fire. I thought I'd bake a little loaf of bread for me and my son. That's all I have. I'm so sorry."

"What will you do for food?" Elijah asked.

"I guess we'll starve." The woman looked so sad.

But Elijah knew God. He knew about God's plan. He knew about God's power. And so he said, "Don't worry about that. Go right in and bake your bread. Then give some to me. There will be enough left for you and your son."

The lady wondered, "But there is so little left."

Elijah knew that God wanted the woman to obey. "Go ahead. The Lord says that there will always be just enough left for you and your son."

The smile slowly came back to her face. "Okay. I will do as you say Elijah." Then she went into her house.

Quickly the woman built a fire. She mixed the flour and oil together and added a few other things. One small loaf was for Elijah. The other small loaf was for herself and her son. The bread smelled so good while it baked. It looked crusty and brown.

The woman peeked into her flour jar. She lifted the lid of the oil jar. And what do you think she saw? Elijah was right! There was enough flour and oil left for tomorrow.

Strange Weapons
(Judges 7:1–8, 15–23)

Gideon and his men were preparing for battle. Their enemy had many good soldiers. So Gideon called together every man he could get and started getting them ready for war. But the Lord looked at Gideon's huge army and said, "Gideon, you have too many men. I want you to tell every man that is afraid to fight to go back home."

Gideon obeyed God. But when he announced this to his men, two out of every three of them left. That's way over half! Now Gideon's army was really quite small.

Again the Lord came to him and said, "Gideon, your army is still far too large. This time I want you to ask the men that are left to go to the water and get a drink. Then I will tell you who should go and who should stay to fight."

Obeying God again, Gideon sent his soldiers to get a drink. Most of them laid down their weapons and bent on their knees to get a drink. Drinking this way took quite a long time. But a few of them quickly bent over and lapped the water with their tongues, just as dogs drink.

Then God said, "Everyone that lapped up the water will stay to fight. All the other soldiers must leave."

Gideon watched closely. Out of every one hundred men, only three stayed! Gideon was left with only three hundred men to fight this important battle. If he wanted to disobey or was afraid to fight with so few men he could have simply forgotten God's command. But Gideon trusted the Lord and started off with three hundred men.

Before they came to the city they were going to fight, Gideon gave every man a trumpet, a pitcher, and a lamp inside each pitcher. Unusual weapons for battle, aren't they? He divided his men into three groups and quietly gave them their orders. Every man knew exactly what he should do and when he should do it.

The groups tiptoed around the city so that there was a group on each side of it. When Gideon gave the signal each man blew his trumpet and smashed his pitcher. Then they took the lamps out and blew the trumpets again. Finally they cried, "The sword of the Lord, and of Gideon."

The people inside the city jumped! What a terrible noise: trumpets blared; something was shattering and crashing and clanging. Suddenly they could see lights on all sides. The trumpets blasted again and then voices shouted, "The sword of the Lord, and of Gideon." It was like a dreadful nightmare!

Terrified by all of this, they ran. Every person in the city jolted up and raced out, hoping to get away safely. They imagined that thousands of soldiers surrounded their city.

Think of it! Only three hundred men with trumpets, lamps, and pitchers. Perhaps they were strange weapons for war, but using these was obeying God. And God gave them the victory.

Acts of
Pride

The Death of a Rich Man

(Luke 16:19–31)

Jesus tells a
story about a
very rich
and a very
proud man.
The rich man
was both of these,
rich and proud. He
wore clothes of
kingly purple
made from fine
linen and expen-
sive silk. Every day he ate very good food.
He was able to buy anything he wanted.

Outside his door lay a poor hungry
man. He was a sick man. Large open sores
covered his body. Stray dogs hung around

him and licked his wounds. He was thrilled if he could even get some of the crumbs or the garbage left from the rich man's meals.

When the rich man went out for a walk, he passed Lazarus, a starving beggar. He put his nose in the air and strutted past. He was too proud to feed him or help him get doctor's care.

One evening both the rich man and Lazarus died. Lazarus went to heaven to be comforted and healed. He lived with God Himself!

But the rich man did not go to heaven. When he had time to think, the rich proud man could understand why he was not allowed to go to heaven. He had been unfriendly and unloving to those he met on earth. He looked up to heaven and cried out in pain, "Please, help me! Come down and give me cool water to drink. I'm burning alive. I can't stand it."

One of God's saints answered back,

"When you were living, you wouldn't help Lazarus, not even once. You had plenty of money. You could have cared for him. But you thought you were too good. Now you are hurting and Lazarus is happy."

A Proud Man Prays
(Luke 18:9–14)

Jesus tells the story about two men who came to the Temple to pray. One was a Pharisee, a church leader. The other man was a publican. That means that he was a tax collector. When the Pharisee strutted up to pray he held his head high in the air. Proudly he looked toward heaven saying, "Dear Lord, I'm so glad that I'm not as bad as other people. They are cheaters, some have many women, and some are tax collectors who actually steal. I fast twice a week. I always give some of my money to the church. Thank you for helping me to be better than other men!"

While the Pharisee prayed, the publican was also talking to God. His hands were folded on his chest. He knew he was a sinner and he wanted God to forgive him. Praying, he asked, "God, be merciful to me. I am a great sinner. Please forgive me." His prayer was very short but he had humbly asked God for something he wanted, a clean heart.

Stop and think for a moment. Which man sounded really sorry for sinning? Did one of the men brag as if he was better than others? Which man stood with bowed head and folded hands?

God heard only one of these prayers. You know now which one it was. He heard the prayer of the tax collector. He knew he was a sinner. The Pharisee prayed as if he was perfect. Not once did he mention any of his sins. He thought he was too important to have to admit to his own wickedness. After all, he was a church leader! But his proud praying was ignored by God.

Who May Throw Stones?
(John 8:1–11)

One afternoon Jesus sat outside writing in the sand. He was thinking as he scribbled. But his thoughts were soon interrupted by a group of people who crowded around Him. They were pulling a woman into the group. They shoved her in front of Jesus and said, "See this woman! What a sinner she is. We caught her living with another man just as if she were married to him!"

They were talking fast because they were so excited. They had caught someone sinning and they had dragged her to Jesus. Finding fault with her was almost like fun. They even wanted to stone her to death!

Jesus completely ignored them. He acted like He was still alone. He continued writing in the sand and thinking.

But the crowd kept pushing the woman and calling, "Lord, don't you understand? This is a very wicked lady. She's done a terrible thing. Aren't you going to do anything to her or say anything at all?" They talked so proudly— just as if they were perfect and never had sinned at all.

The woman blushed, because she was embarrassed. The crowd was right. She had sinned and they had caught her living in another man's house. Nervously she waited, wondering what would happen to her.

Finally Jesus said to the crowd. "Any one of you that is perfect, has never done

one sin, may throw the first stone." Then He looked down again and continued writing in the sand. The crowd quieted down. Each one was looking into his own heart. They each saw a lot of very bad sins inside themselves. Jesus had said that only the perfect ones could throw stones. One by one they silently left. They were ashamed. How proud they had been to think they were so good. They had no right to pick on someone who was no worse than they were.

In a short time everyone had left. The woman stood alone with Jesus. He got up and said to her, "I will not stone you either. Go now, and sin no more."

Deeds of
Humility

An Empty Pocketbook
(Mark 12:41–44)

Have you ever heard the word *humble?* Do you know what it means? It isn't hard to understand. It means the opposite of proud. A humble person doesn't brag and talk about how good he is or how much he can do. He does his good works quietly and sincerely.

There was a woman who was a widow, for her husband was dead. She lived alone and had very little money to live on. But she loved Jesus so much that she always saved out enough to bring to the Temple to help in the Lord's work.

One day she put on her better clothes and walked to the Temple. In her hand she held two mites. The coins were worth less than one penny in our money. You know that isn't very much, but it was all the money she had to bring.

When she came to the Temple, other people were dropping coins into the money box. One man was especially rich. His clothes were satin and velvet. He walked up to the box with a large bag of coins and poured in the whole bag of money. With a satisfied look he slowly walked away.

The widow knew that she had very little to give. She hurried up to the box, almost hoping no one would notice her. Quickly she dropped in her two small coins and hurried home. She wished that she had more to give.

Jesus saw both of these people, the rich and the poor. He told his friends that the widow had given far more than anyone.

Surprised, Jesus' friends said, "Wait a minute. How can that be? The poor widow dropped in two small coins. The rich man gave a whole bag full. Certainly the man gave more!"

"You're wrong," Jesus answered. "The rich man has many more money bags at home. He won't even miss the one he gave today. But the widow doesn't have even one penny left. She gave everything, every single penny she had. Indeed, she did give more!"

Father, Forgive Me!
(Luke 15:11–24)

With his money in his pocket and his clothes in a suitcase, a young man set out to live by himself. He left his older brother and father at home.

He wanted to live alone, so he could do exactly what he wanted to do.

He asked his father to divide the money that he and his brother would get someday. He took his half and proudly hurried off to see the world and have some fun!

In the first city he stopped, he rented an expensive apartment with fancy furniture. He hustled to the grocery store and bought bags of tasty but costly food. He invited people over to his house. He wanted friends and parties, lots of both!

Night after night he used his time and money this way. During the days he slept so he could feel wide awake for the night-time parties. "When did he work?" you ask. He didn't, and so his money was used up quite quickly.

When he had no money left, he went out to find a job. His friends left him. He wasn't any good to them now because he didn't have a cent. He couldn't rent the apartment and couldn't buy any food. He needed a job very badly.

But jobs were pretty hard to get. The country was having a bad year. The crops had not grown. There was little to eat. Few people could afford to hire another worker.

At last he had to be happy with the best job he could find—feeding pigs. He waded through the slop to throw corn to them. He slept in the fields near them. Every second he smelled their dirtiness. The pigs stayed roly-poly on the dried corn, but he was starving. His stomach growled so long and loud that he almost wanted to eat pig's food.

While he sat in the mud and filth he thought to himself, "How stupid of me. I thought I was so smart to leave home. I wanted to be a big shot. Ha! Look at me ... feeding pigs. Some big shot I turned out to be! I wasted all my money and now I'm starving to death. Even my Dad's servants have more than I've got. Hmmm ... home ... dad .... good food — that's what I'll do. I'm going back to my father's house. I'll fall on my knees and beg his forgiveness."

As soon as he made the decision he jumped up and headed for home. His father noticed him coming in the distance and ran out to welcome him calling, "My son! My son! How happy I am to see you again!"

The runaway son fell on his knees and humbly asked his father to forgive him. Of course the happy father was thrilled to see him and forgave him immediately. His lost son was home at last!

Acts of
Dishonesty

A Trick on Father

(Genesis 27:1–40)

Isaac was growing old and was going blind. He didn't know how much longer he'd live. So he called Esau, his older son, and said, "Go out and kill a deer. Bring the meat home and make me a bowl of stew, the tasty kind you make so well. Then I'll give you your blessing." Isaac wanted to do it soon because he was so old. He had no idea how long God would leave him on this earth.

Rebekah, Isaac's wife, heard Isaac talking to Esau. She wanted Jacob, the younger son, to get the blessing. Quickly she called Jacob in and told him, "Run out and kill two baby goats. I'll fix the spicy stew your father likes. Then you can give it to your father. You will have the blessing instead of Esau."

But Jacob wasn't so sure about this trick. He said, "But Mom, Dad will know the difference. Esau's arms are hairy and mine aren't. Besides he knows our voices. We sound different when we talk."

"Go and do what I've told you," Rebekah ordered him. "You must get the blessing. I will help you."

Jacob killed the baby goats and Rebekah made the stew. She put the goat skin on Jacob's arms and neck. Jacob put on some of Esau's clothes. Then he walked into his father's room, hoping the trick would work.

Isaac, hearing someone come into his room, asked, "Who is it?"

Jacob lied, "I am Esau, your older son. I am back with your stew. It's nice and hot and ready to eat, just the way you like it."

But Isaac suspected something. He said, "Come closer so I can touch you." He couldn't see the difference because his eyes were so weak and blurry. He hoped he could feel the difference.

When he touched Jacob's arms he said, "You sound like Jacob. But you feel like Esau." He rubbed his wrinkled, shaky hands over the skins. Then he added, "Are you really my son Esau?"

Jacob answered, "Yes, I am. I am."

Convinced at last, Isaac ate the stew and then raised his arms over Jacob to bless him. "You will be a rich man. You'll have all the food you can eat. You will be important. Many people will respect you and look up to you. God will stay with you always."

Jacob hurried off, happy that he had the blessing. He and his mother had to be dishonest to get it. Both of them stole the blessing from Esau, and Jacob also lied.

Seven Times Two

(Genesis 29:15–28)

Jacob hurried away from home because he was so afraid. Esau was furious with him for stealing his blessing. Esau even wanted to kill him. So Jacob rushed off to visit his Uncle Laban, who lived far away.

When he arrived at his uncle's house he was happy . . . happy to be away from Esau and happy with what he saw at Uncle Laban's. Laban had a daughter named Rachel. She was a very beautiful girl. Since Jacob was ready to marry, he naturally wanted Rachel for his wife. He fell deeply in love with her.

Jacob went to Laban and offered, "I will work for you for seven years if I may marry Rachel."

Laban agreed. Seven years of work would be a big help. And the work would be free! Jacob would be working to pay for or to buy Rachel for his wife.

Those years flew by because Jacob was eager to marry Rachel. He loved her so dearly. He thought how they'd set up their own house, get their own flocks, and have a family. In no time at all, those seven years were past.

The day of the wedding came. Can't you imagine Jacob's excitement? The bride walked in with a wedding veil that covered her face. That's the kind they wore in that country.

When the wedding was over Jacob and his new wife went home. When Jacob took off her veil he was shocked! He blinked his eyes. "Can it be true?" he asked himself. "Uncle Laban has given me Leah, Rachel's older sister! Oh, no!"

Jacob raced back to Laban and demanded, "I worked seven years to marry Rachel. But you've given me Leah. You tricked me. You've lied."

Of course Laban knew what he had done. He had been dishonest. He said,

"Jacob, in our country the oldest must marry first. Now that Leah is married you may marry Rachel if you wish. But you must work another seven years for her."

Jacob agreed to this because he loved Rachel so. He married Rachel, but he had to work another seven years. Altogether he worked fourteen years to marry the girl he loved.

(1 Kings 3:16–28)

Throughout the kingdom King Solomon was known for his wisdom. Whenever there was a difficult problem, people came to him. He was a great problem solver!

One day two women came into his throne room. They were screaming and arguing. They were fighting over something that one of the women was carrying. The King was quite surprised when he saw they were fighting over a baby!

"Quiet down, ladies," he said to them. "One at a time. Who would like to speak first?"

One of them began, "Last night we both went to bed with our babies. During the night she rolled over on hers and the baby died. Then she took my live baby and put the dead one by me."

Almost before she had finished talking the other woman started, "Oh, no! That's not how it happened at all! You rolled over on yours and gave me the dead baby. The live one is mine!"

In a moment they were fussing at each other again. King Solomon ordered them to be quiet for the second time. He wanted a little time to think. This wasn't an easy problem. A little baby is a very precious thing. He had to be certain to give it to the right mother. But how would he know? How would he know?

When he reached his decision he said, "Guards, bring a sword. We'll cut the baby in half so each of you may have half of it."

Everyone in the throne room looked surprised. Are you? Would Solomon really cut the baby in half? King Solomon was just testing the women. He wouldn't really do it. But the baby's true mother believed him. She was horrified! "Kill my baby," she cried, "never! Give him to the other lady. Then at least he will be alive!"

The mother of the dead baby didn't care. The live baby wasn't hers anyway. So she said, "That's a good idea. That'll be fair. We'll each have half."

Now King Solomon knew which was the real mother. She was the one that didn't want the baby to be hurt. He gave her the living baby and she hurried home to care for it.

Two Lies and Two Deaths
(Acts 5:1–11)

When Christ's church began hundreds of years ago, the people were very generous. They gave a lot of money to help each other, and they did it willingly.

Ananias and Sapphira, a married couple, owned some land. They sold it to be able to give more money to the church. But before they brought it they saved some of it out for themselves.

Ananias went to the church leaders first. He brought his wallet with him. When he took the money out and gave it to them, he said, "My wife and I sold some of our land. We're giving all the money to the church."

Peter, the church leader, knew he was lying. God had told him. Peter spoke to Ananias, "Why are you lying? You're obeying Satan. You have really saved part of the money for yourselves."

As soon as Peter said that, Ananias crumpled over in a heap on the floor. He died immediately. The church leaders took him outside and buried him.

About three hours later, Sapphira walked into the church. She was looking for her husband, Ananias. He'd been gone so long.

Peter saw her and asked, "Sapphira, did you and your husband sell some land? And are you giving all of the money to the church?"

"Yes," she quickly answered. She knew that she and her husband had agreed to lie about it. "My husband brought the money to you, didn't he?"

"You're right," Peter said. "But why did you and Ananias agree to lie? The same men who buried your husband will also bury you." No sooner had Peter spoken when Sapphira wilted to the floor, dead!

You may think that God was too strict with Ananias and Sapphira. After all, we don't have to give all of our money, do we? The answer is No. But their sin was lying. They should have told Peter that they sold their land and were bringing part of the money to the Lord. But they were dishonest.

Sins of
Idolatry

Worshiping a Calf

(Exodus 32:1–6, 19–29)

Do you know if you have ever seen an idol? Do you know what is meant by an idol? It is anything you worship or the thing that you love most of all. Clothes and money are idols for some people. It is all they can think about. Others use new cars as idols. Some have little figures or statues that they worship instead of God. Christians may not have idols. We are to worship God and love Him above everything else.

While Moses was leading the Israelites out of Egypt, the people fell into the sin of idolatry. God had called Moses up to a mountaintop so He could talk with him. Moses was with God for a very long time.

The Israelites thought that Moses wasn't coming back.

They came crying to Aaron, "Moses is surely gone for good. He'll never come back. We need something to worship! Aaron, will you please make us some gods?"

Aaron really knew better. He knew that it is sinful to worship statues or idols. But instead he said, "Bring all of your earrings to me . . . all the nice golden dangling ones that your wives and your children wear. I will make you a beautiful golden statue for your worship. It will be your god who brought you out of the land of Egypt."

The people scattered quickly. They went from tent to tent collecting earrings. They filled baskets full of them. When the last earring was gathered they brought the collection to Aaron.

Carefully he melted the jewelry over a hot fire. Then he shaped it into the figure of an animal. He carved and chiseled until it looked exactly like a calf... a golden calf! He polished it until it glittered in the sun. Then he placed it in front of the people.

As soon as they saw their glistening idol, their new god, they liked it. They made sacrifices and bowed low before their golden god. Imagine! People praying to a chunk of gold as if it could hear them! How silly and sinful these grown-ups were acting!

God could see what His people were doing. He was angry with them. It seemed to Him that they would never learn—that they would never really turn away from sinning.

Moses saw it too. He hurried down the steep slopes. In his hands he held two tablets of stone. God Himself had written the Ten Commandments on these heavy tablets. As Moses came closer and closer to the bottom of the mountain, the more disgusted he became. Finally he flung the stone tablets in anger. They lay on the ground in bits and pieces.

Later Moses burned the golden calf until it melted. And when it was cool, he ground it into a fine powder. Slowly he sprinkled it over the water and made the people drink it.

I don't know what the ashes of burnt gold would taste like. But I can imagine that they must have choked and gagged on it. Later three thousand people who had worshiped the idol were punished. God's own people should have known better than to worship an idol!

A Contest

(1 Kings 18:17–40)

Baal was worshiped by some of the people in King Ahab's country. They built altars to this god and made statues of him. But others honored God, the only true Lord. And so it went—the people kept arguing about who was truly God Himself. Some worshiped the true God; others didn't.

In this land there was a prophet of God named Elijah. He wanted to show the people that God alone should be loved, that

He is the only true God. Elijah asked King Ahab to send the prophets of Baal to Mount Carmel. He had something special in mind.

There were four hundred and fifty prophets of Baal that came. Elijah was the only prophet of God. Together they climbed this mountain while the people followed closely behind.

When all the prophets and people reached the top of Mount Carmel Elijah announced, "Today we're going to find out which god is truly God. Men, bring two little bulls for the sacrifice. You prophets of Baal, build an altar to Baal. I'll build one for my God. Then we'll both ask our gods to send fire from heaven to burn our sacrifices. Whichever god does that will be named God of all."

The prophets of Baal agreed. They built their altar, put the sacrifice on top, and called to Baal. "Oh, Baal, hear us! Send fire to show that you are God."

While they called they kept dancing. They thought that their god would surely hear and see them.

All morning this continued. They sang and danced and called to Baal. But Baal wasn't answering them. Elijah began to tease them a little, ''Maybe Baal is on his vacation. Or he may be napping. Perhaps if you will call a little louder, he just might wake up.''

The prophets of Baal were getting very worried about their god. Where could he be? They cried louder. They danced faster. They shouted and screamed. Oh, how badly they wanted Baal to answer them.

When evening finally came, there was no fire to burn Baal's sacrifice. He had not heard them. He hadn't answered them because Baal was only an idol. He was not God at all.

Then Elijah called the people around him. He built an altar from twelve stones.

He put a ditch around it. He cut the little bull in pieces and put them on the altar. Then he poured many buckets of water over the altar until it was soaked and the ditch was full.

The people watched him, wondering, "Why did he soak the altar? Doesn't he know that anything wet will not burn? How can any god burn a dripping wet altar?"

Elijah stood before the people and prayed to God, "Dear Lord, let the people know that you are the only true God. Send fire from heaven to burn this sacrifice. Then they will worship you as the only true God."

Silently everyone waited. They wondered if they would have to wait another whole day as they did for Baal. Elijah wasn't dancing around. He wasn't shouting. He stood prayerfully and trusted the Lord to answer him.

Before the people realized what had happened, fire shot from heaven like falling stars. It snapped and crackled as it ate up the meat and drank the water. Yes, even that sopping wet altar was licked until it was black and dry!

The people were amazed. They were shocked. They fell down on their knees and worshiped God. They knew for certain that Baal wasn't God. At last they knew and believed the true God. The prophets of Baal were captured and punished for their idolatry.

Living for Money

(Luke 18:18–23)

A young ruler came to Jesus and asked, "Good teacher, what do I have to do to go to heaven when I die?"

Jesus answered, "You must obey all the commandments. Be careful not to kill. Never steal or tell a lie. And always be kind to your mom and dad."

A smile flashed across his face when he heard that. He spoke quickly, "I've done all of that. I do keep the commandments. I'm very careful about that. I have kept all the commandments ever since I was a boy."

"But there's one more thing," Jesus added. "You must sell all your belongings and give your money, all of it, to the poor people. Then you will go to heaven."

The smile dropped from his face as thoughts galloped through his mind. "Give away all my things?" he asked himself. "I can't do it. I'm too rich. If I did that I'd be a beggar. I could never give away all my clothes or sell my brand-new house. Besides I've saved a lot of money. I couldn't stand to give it away." Without saying any more to Jesus he turned and trudged toward home. He wasn't willing to do that for heaven!

Why did Jesus tell him to give away everything he had? Jesus didn't say that because all God's people must do it in order to go to heaven. He said it because He knew this rich man loved his money; it was his idol. It meant more to him than going to heaven. The rich man kept his idols but he missed the glory of living forever with God!

Jesus Is
Coming Again

Watching for Jesus

(Matthew 24:36–42; Acts 1:11)

You have read stories about many kinds of sins. You have also read about people who pleased God. If you are one of God's children, you will always try to obey Him. You will look for that day when Jesus will come again. Won't that be marvelous! Every dead person will be raised from his or her grave. Every living person, every one of them, will watch Jesus floating down from the clouds. This is the very important day all Christians are waiting for.

But what should we do until then? The Bible tells us to watch for Him. What does that mean? Should you stop playing with your friends or quit going to school?

Should your dad quit his job? Should your family go to the top of a mountain and watch the sky for this exciting day? Just what does the Bible mean when it tells us to watch?

God wants us to watch with our hearts, not our eyes. He certainly doesn't want us to twiddle our thumbs and watch the clouds, because no one knows when that day will be. It would be wasting our time to sit and wait. He wants us to be anxious for that day. He wants us to hope for it. It should be the day that we're most eager for . . . more excited for it than for our next birthday or Christmas or anything at all. Jesus wants us to have our hearts ready to greet Him.

Learning About Jesus
(2 Timothy 2:15)

Is it enough to have our hearts ready for Him? No, we must do more. We must

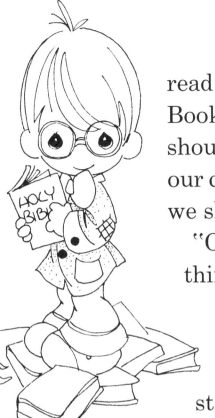

read the Bible, God's Book. It tells us how we should live. It answers our questions about what we should do.

"Oh, dear," you're thinking. "I can't read the Bible. It's too hard. Sometimes I don't even understand it. There are so many big words in it."

There's something you can do instead, at least until you're old enough to read it yourself. You should listen carefully when someone does read the Bible. Listen and try to understand. Some of the stories you'll know. Listen for new things. Listen to them on the radio or on records, and in Sunday school. Maybe you can't use your eyes to read, but you can use your ears to listen.

There's one more thing God tells us about reading or listening to the Bible. We must believe it. God is telling us very special things that He wrote for us to hear. We must never think, "Oh, that couldn't be true." God wrote the whole Bible. He would never write a lie. It is all truth and we must believe it.

Talking with Jesus
(Matthew 6:5–6; Mark 11:24–25)

We must also pray to Jesus. Praying is talking to God and listening carefully in your heart for Him to talk to you.

Just what should you talk about when

you do talk to Him? Tell Him exactly what is on your mind. When you're happy, tell Him and tell Him why. He likes us to be happy people. If you're sad, tell Him and tell Him why. Ask Him for help. If you've been naughty, ask Him to take that sin away. Thank Him for all the good things He gives you.

You probably want to know if you should ask Him for things. The answer is Yes. If you really need something, ask

Him for it. Maybe you want a dog or a new tricycle or a two-wheeler. Should you ask Him for it? You don't really need it, but you'd like to have it.

Certainly you may ask for these things. But always remember that there are two answers, Yes and No. If God answers Yes, thank Him for giving it to you. If He answers No, thank Him for hearing your prayer, even though He answered No. Remember God always does what is best for you.

Where should you pray? When should you pray? You may pray in any place and at any time . . . on the playground, in your bedroom, before you eat, while you're doing the dishes, or any other time. Usually we fold our hands and close our eyes to show God that we honor Him. In your bedroom you might pray on your knees. But if you want to talk to Jesus at other times, just close your eyes a minute and whisper a little message to Him. If you believe on Him, He will hear all your prayers. Always remember to pray!

Living for Jesus

(Matthew 5:43–48)

Jesus also wants us to be very busy working for Him. He also wants us to show our love to others. If we really have this love in our hearts we can show it in so many ways!

One way is by being happy. Smile around the house. Whistle or sing a little tune. But be very careful about that grumbling! That is Satan's work. Whenever you're tempted to say bad things, don't!

Push Satan out of your heart. Ask God to help you.

If one of your friends is sick, make him a get well card. Take it over to his house or send it through the mail.

Visit Grandma and Grandpa if you have them. They love to see their grandchildren. Cheer them up by coming into the house with a big smile on your face.

Be careful when you're playing. Be kind to your friends. God wants you to take turns. Share your things. Never cry and shout just because you didn't get what you wanted. God doesn't want his little Christians to be stingy.

Help your mom and dad. Sometimes they're so busy and get pretty tired. Put on a smile and offer to help clean the garage or help put the clothes away.

Be careful how you speak. Always do it quietly and kindly. Don't scream and holler. It's so much more pleasant to hear people speaking softly, isn't it? If you are careful not to shout when you speak to others, they will be careful not to holler at you.

Can you think of more ways to show love and kindness?

Telling About Jesus
(Mark 16:15–16)

There's one more thing. You must tell other children about Jesus and how He loves little children.

Tell the little boy or girl who lives next door or down the street a little ways. Or better yet, take your friend along with you when you go to Sunday school. Maybe you have a Bible story book or a tape you could lend. Then he or she can listen to these stories at home too.

Always be ready to talk about Jesus. If we love Him as much as we say we do, then we'll just have to tell others. This is a very important part of being a Christian boy or girl or mother or father.

Now stop and think of all the things you and I must do until Jesus comes again . . . watch for Him with our hearts, read the Bible, pray, show kindness to others, and tell the good news about Jesus. That's quite a list, isn't it? It will keep us very busy if we are really doing all of these things for our Lord. Isn't it wonderful to believe in Jesus!

Friends
and Play

A Special Birthday

Laura had saved a very special present to open last. It was a birthday present from Grandma and Grandpa. They almost always got her a doll, but she had no idea what was in this tiny box. She sat down with her two favorite dolls and opened her last present.

It was a beautiful music box! Laura

lifted the top and laughed when she heard the little song.

"What is this?" she asked her dolls. They just smiled back at her as she took a little card out of the box.

Two ten-dollar bills fell out! There was also a little note that said:

> Dear Laura,
> We wanted to buy you a doll, but we didn't know which one you would like. So this birthday we want you to get a very special doll, one that you can keep for your own little girl.
>
> Love, Grandma
> and Grandpa

Laura was excited. She knew just which doll she wanted. There was one little girl doll at the toy store that she liked so very much. She looked at the money again and said, "Mom, with this money I can buy *two* dolls—one for me and one for my best friend Becky."

"Maybe you should think about that a little more, Laura. Grandma and Grandpa want you to have a very special doll. Maybe you'll find one."

"But, Mom, if I buy two of them, both Becky and I will have a special doll. She would like to have a new doll too. The only one she has is one her sister played with."

"Hi! Laura!" called Becky. "May I see your presents?"

Becky and Laura looked at the music box and the other nice gifts.

"Becky, I'm so excited! With my birthday money I can buy *two* dolls, one for you and one for me. Just think of the fun we're going to have."

"Well, Laura, I think you should get just one doll, the prettiest one you can find. That's your birthday money and you should use it for yourself," said Becky. "We can take turns playing with her. I know you have a favorite doll picked out at the toy store."

"C'mon!" said Laura. "Let's go to the store now."

The best friends skipped along, happy

to be together. They looked in the window of the toy store and saw so many wonderful toys—stuffed animals, blocks, even a Jack-in-the-box. In one corner of the window was a beautiful baby doll just waiting for a new mother.

"Isn't she pretty?" gasped Laura. "She must have just come in."

"She's adorable!!" agreed Becky. "Let's go in and see if we can hold her."

Laura picked up the doll and cuddled her. "Mm-m-m! I'd like to take you home! I'll call you Baby Sue."

Laura and Becky took turns carrying Baby Sue around as the two friends looked at all the other dolls in the store. Both agreed that none of the other dolls was as pretty as little Baby Sue.

"It looks like Baby Sue is the one for you," said Becky, who was just a little sad that Laura had enough money for only *one* Baby Sue.

Laura smiled at the doll. "I'm going to put you back in your corner, Baby Sue. But, maybe I'll come back for you."

"Why didn't you buy Baby Sue, Laura?" asked Becky.

"I want to talk to my mom first," said Laura, with a twinkle in her eye. "C'mon, I'll race you home."

That night Laura and her Mother talked a long time about Baby Sue and Becky.

"Mom, Becky is too proud to say she'd like a Baby Sue of her own. But I saw the look in her eye as she held her. Becky has only one worn-out doll. I just wouldn't be happy playing with Baby Sue, even if I shared her with Becky, because I know Becky would love to have a doll of her own. I wish I could give Becky a Baby Sue. . . but I want a Baby Sue, too."

"Hmmm," said Mother. "Maybe there is a way to solve this problem. I want to

think about it tonight. Let's pray about it. Now you go to sleep. Sweet dreams!"

Laura could see that Mother had a special surprise sparkle in her eyes the next morning but Mother wouldn't tell her the happy secret.

"Let's check the toy store today," said Laura when Becky came over to play that afternoon.

Together the friends skipped to the store. They looked for Baby Sue's corner in the window and. . . SHE WASN'T THERE!!!

"Maybe they moved her," said Becky. "We could look inside."

Whoosh! They opened the door and ran to the doll section. No Baby Sue!

"She's gone! I wonder if someone bought her! What will we do now?" cried Laura.

Slowly the two friends walked back to Laura's house. They had very sad faces and once in a while a tear came down a cheek.

Becky snuffed back a sob.

Laura snuffed back two sobs.

They were VERY sad! Mother was waiting for the two friends. She was wearing her special surprise smile and even her eyes were sparkling.

"Come in, girls! There's a surprise in the den," she said, with that special smile.

"Nothing, NOTHING!!! Not even a surprise could make us happy today, Mom," cried Laura.

"Oh, why?" asked Mother.

"Baby Sue is gone! She's not at the toy store," Becky sobbed.

"Really?" said Mother, who didn't sound at all surprised to hear that news.

There were two packages in the corner of the den. They were exactly alike, except one said, "TO BECKY." The other one said, "TO LAURA."

"Okay," said Mother. "Unwrap them together.

O-N-E, T-W-O, THREE, GO!"

Rustle, rustle, rustle! Then no sound at all, not even a breathing sound. Laura lifted a baby doll out of her box. Becky lifted a baby doll out of *her* box.

"Baby Sue!" said Laura.

"Oh, look at this," cried Becky, "I have a Baby Sue, too."

Both of the girls giggled with delight.

"I know, Becky, let's call yours Baby Lu and call mine Baby Sue," Laura said with a big smile.

Now it was Mother's turn to wipe a tear off her cheek. But it was a happy tear.

The Echo

Johnny was lonesome, VERY LONE-
SOME!!! He and his mother and father
had just moved to the country. There were
some dandy hills and some exciting caves
in the hills near the river. It was almost a
perfectly nice place to live. But Johnny
had no one to play with. NO ONE!!! This
made Johnny sad, super sad. Today he

was mighty sad and very lonesome. It just wasn't a good day for Johnny.

He climbed to the top of the hill to see if

there was anyone around to play with. No, Johnny couldn't see any boys. He couldn't see any girls. He couldn't see any dogs. He couldn't see any kittens. He was alone on the hill. He couldn't find anyone!

"I wonder if there is another boy on the top of that hill over there. It's too far away to see anybody. Maybe if I yell, somebody will hear me," Johnny said to himself.

Johnny took a deep breath and yelled as loud as he could, "H-E-L-L-O!"

To his surprise, he heard, "H-e-l-l-o!" from across the valley.

"Well, what do you know about that?" Johnny chuckled. "There is a little boy over there on the top of that hill and he sounds like he's about my age."

"How are you?" Johnny called.

"How are you?" came back from across the valley.

"I'm fine," Johnny answered. "How are you?"

"I'm fine. How are you?"

"I already said I'm fine," Johnny screamed.

"I already said I'm fine," came back from across the valley.

"Hmm-mm," Johnny said softly, almost to himself, "I wonder what kind of a boy is over there. Every time I call to him, he says the very same thing back to me. Is he trying to play some kind of game with me?"

"Hey, are you trying to be funny?" Johnny snapped.

"Hey, are you trying to be funny?" came back from across the valley.

"OK, wise guy, I'm coming over to fix you good!" Johnny bellowed.

"OK, wise guy, I'm coming over to fix you good!" was the reply.

Johnny's face got red. He was angry. He thought of some not-so-nice things to say to that "kid" on the next hill. "Oh, oh,

what if he's bigger than I am? What if he's
a great big guy? What if he's ten feet tall?"

Johnny was SCARED. He was really

scared. Suddenly he ran down the hill, stormed into the house, and scrambled under the blanket on his bed.

"Why, Johnny!" said Mother. "What on earth is wrong?"

"It's that kid on the other hill, Mom. I was trying to be friendly to him when all of a sudden he started saying bad things to me."

"Hmm-m that's strange. Are you sure you didn't start saying bad things to him first?" Mother asked.

"No, Mom, I'm really sure. He started it," said Johnny, just peeking out from under the blanket.

"Well, I have an idea," Mother said. "Let's go to the hill again and I'll listen while you tell that boy you are sorry that you said mean things to him."

"I can't do that, Mom," Johnny cried. "You don't understand. He's bigger than I am and he will never make up with me."

"C'mon, I'll go with you," said Mother. "Let's go now. We'll just give it a try."

Slowly Johnny crawled out from under his blanket. He didn't want to climb that hill and talk to that big mean kid again.

He'd had enough hassle from him for one day. In fact, he didn't want to talk to that kid for a long time—maybe never. Johnny would rather be sad and lonesome than to talk to that meanie. But Johnny knew he had to obey his mother. So off they went.

Johnny's knees knocked as he slowly walked to the top of the hill. Mother was walking with him but that didn't help one bit—well, maybe only a little bit. When they reached the top, Johnny looked over the valley and then slowly looked at the great big hill on the other side. He stared at the bottom of the hill and then slowly looked up the hill to the very top.

"I sure hope that he's not mad any-more," Johnny whispered to himself. "Anyway, now that I'm up here I may as well do what Mother said."

"I'm very sorry," Johnny said, not nearly as loud as the first time he talked to the "big mean kid."

"I'm very sorry," the voice replied.

"I can't believe it, Mom," Johnny said. "He's sorry too."

"Do you want to be my friend?" Johnny asked.

"Do you want to be my friend?" the voice replied.

"Yes, I want to be your friend," Johnny shouted.

"Yes, I want to be your friend," the voice shouted back.

Mom and Johnny hugged each other as Johnny said, "Mom! Now I've found a new friend. That kid over there isn't angry with me anymore."

Mother just smiled at Johnny.

"You see," she said, "being nice to someone is the best way to make a friend."

Mother didn't tell Johnny the secret about the echo. They were going to talk about that when she tucked him in at bedtime.

Yen Finds a Friend

"Grandfather is here," Yen's mother said, peeking into the kitchen where Yen was eating his breakfast.

Yen had just moved to America from halfway across the world. All of his friends were in China, far, far away, and Yen was very LONELY. But today was a very special day. Grandfather was going to take him to the zoo. Yen had never been to a zoo and he was very excited.

"Hello, Grandfather," the little boy said. Grandfather gave Yen a big hug.

"I've missed you, Yen. I have a present for you on this special day," said Grandfather.

Yen tore off the paper. Inside was a bright red T-shirt. The white letters on the front and back said USA.

"Oh, thank you, Grandfather," the little boy said. "I'm going to wear it today. I'll be back in just a minute after I change shirts."

When Yen and Grandfather got to the zoo, the first thing they saw was a big animal with strange skin. It looked like the skin that shoes are made of.

"He's so big, Grandfather," said Yen. "What is his name? The words on the sign look almost as big as he is."

"That's a rhinoceros!" said Grandfather. "You will see many more strange animals here. Look over there. Do you know what that one is called?"

Yen shook his head. "Well, she has a big pocket in front. Is she called some kind of pocket?"

"No," said Grandfather. "She is a kangaroo. The pouch in front is where she carries her baby. A kangaroo baby is called a joey. Kangaroos come from Australia. That's even farther away than China."

"I wonder if she's lonely. She left all her friends in Australia," said Yen sadly.

Yen's grandfather smiled and gave Yen a big hug. "She doesn't look lonely to me. I think I see a smile on her face. She's made many new friends here.

"See that blue bird? He's singing a song just for her. And there

is another kangaroo. Over there are some
bunnies just waiting to play with her. I
think she likes her new home."

They walked down a path and came to
a sign that said GIRAFFE BARN. There
were tall trees and long grass.

Yen pointed to an animal with a very,

very long neck. "Where did this animal live, Grandfather?"

"Let's see, I think he came from Africa," said Grandfather. "He probably lived close to the elephants that we just passed. Maybe they were neighbors in Africa and that's why the zoo keeper made them neighbors here. Doesn't that giraffe look happy? I think he likes his home."

"Getting hungry, Yen?" asked Grandfather. "Are you ready for a snack?"

"Yes, I am, Grandfather," said Yen. "That sign says POPCORN. Let's try some of it!"

"Good choice," said Grandfather, as he bought some popcorn.

Yen and Grandfather sat on a bench to rest because Grandfather wanted to talk with Yen. "Sometimes," Grandfather said, "you can feel very lonely in a new place. But now that we've seen how happy the animals are in their new home with

their new friends, maybe you can understand that you can be happy in a new place, too.

"You know," Grandfather said, "one day I read a story in the Bible about some very lonely men. They were friends of Jesus and they thought Jesus was going to go away and leave them. Jesus knew how lonely they felt. You see, once he was so lonely, too. He didn't have any friends. Every friend had left him because they were afraid.

"Jesus knew that there was only one way to cheer up his friends. He made a special promise: 'I will never leave you. I will always be with you.'

"Yen, Jesus has promised me this, too. And he will give you the same promise if you believe him. He will always be your BEST FRIEND. And I believe he will also soon give you some special friends. Let's talk to Jesus by praying to him now. We'll ask him to be your special friend and to give you new friends and help you to be happy in your new home."

Yen felt much better after their little talk.

"Now, I know that sometimes you will miss some things you had in your old home. That's why I want you to meet a very special animal. C'mon, I'll introduce you."

Now Yen was excited. Who could Grandfather be talking about? Who would want to be Yen's special animal? They walked all the way to the other side of the zoo. Finally they stopped at a large bamboo grove. And rolling on the ground was. . .

"A PANDA!" Yen shouted. "Oh, Grandfather, he came all the way from China, just like me!"

The fuzzy little black and white panda looked up at Yen and seemed to smile.

Then he got up and walked over close to where Yen was watching.

"Smile, Yen, please," said a big man who seemed to come from nowhere. "I want to take a picture of the two of you. In fact, I'll take two pictures, one for me and one for you. I have a special kind of camera and you can have your very own picture in just a minute."

So Yen smiled, a

VERY BIG SMILE. And the panda walked even closer to Yen.

Snap! Snap!

"Here's your picture," said the man. "It's a good one. Both of you seem to like each other."

"Thanks, Sir," said Yen. "Thank you so much."

Yen put the picture on the bulletin board in his bedroom. Soon that special picture was surrounded by pictures of smiling boys and girls—Yen's new friends. You see, he did make new friends just as Grandfather had promised.

Family
Times

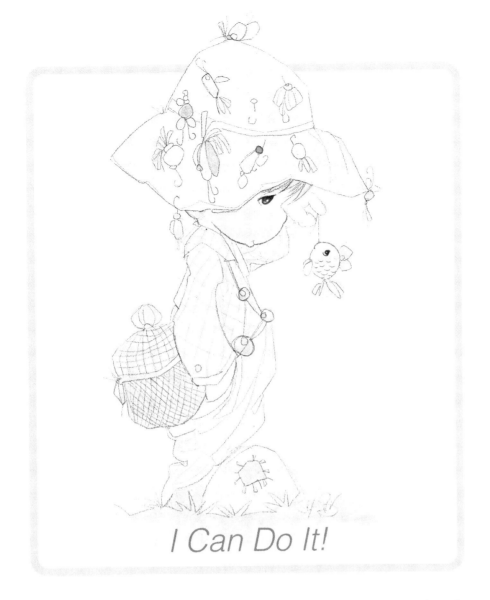

I Can Do It!

"What do you think, Grandpa?" asked Timmy. "Will we catch lots of fish today?"

The pond was sparkling as it caught the bright sun's rays. The birds were singing, happy to be out on such a sunny day.

"Sure, Timmy," said Grandpa. "Some days are just made for fishing. . . and this is one of them."

Splash! a fish had jumped. Then another. . . and another. There really were big ones in the pond.

Timmy was a new fisherman and Grandpa showed him how to tie on a hook and then a small sinker. Next Timmy slipped a red-and-white bobber on his line so he could tell when a fish nibbled at the worm. Putting a wiggly, slippery worm on the hook was hard and Grandpa made Timmy try again and again until he had it on just right.

"OK, fish! Now I'm ready!" said Timmy. He waited for a big whopper to bite. But nothing happened.

"Hey," said Grandpa, "I've got one!" And he did, a beautiful bluegill. He soon caught a sunfish, then another bluegill.

Timmy began to feel sad because he hadn't caught any fish and Grandpa already had three. Suddenly the red-and-white bobber took a nose dive. Timmy had a fish on his line. He jerked the pole and began to bring the fish to shore. He just knew this was a B-I-G one! Timmy's eyes lit up and his muscles bulged.

Snap!! the fish spit out the hook. Splash!!! the fish fell back into the pond.

There was nothing left but a limp line, a shiny hook, and a very sad Timmy.

"Grandpa, I lost him! I'm no good at anything." Timmy tried hard not to cry.

"Aw, Timmy, I'm sorry your fish got away. I lose a lot of fish, too. It happens all the time. Try again."

Timmy baited the hook and threw out
the line. TUG! Sure enough, there was a

fish on his line. Timmy became so excited that he waved his arms and spun around a couple of times. He just wasn't very good at pulling fish in. Timmy became all tangled up in the line and the little fish landed on top of Timmy's head. The fish was much too small to keep.

"Grandpa, I'm just NO GOOD AT ANYTHING!!!" Timmy sighed loudly.

Grandpa put his arm around Timmy's shoulders.

"Timmy, do you know that everyone is good at something? All you have to do is find out what you're good at and then have fun working at it."

"Really, Grandpa? What do you think I would be good at?"

"Well, I'm not sure. When King David of Israel was a little boy, he loved to shoot a sling. He practiced with his sling every day. When he became older, he used a sling to kill a mighty giant. But as great

a warrior as David was, he could also play the harp better than anyone else in his whole kingdom."

"Well, I'm not good with a slingshot, either," Timmy confessed. "But I can play the guitar a little bit."

"So there you are," said Grandpa, as he gave Timmy a hug. "And I know you can play even better. All it takes is time and practice."

"Whoops! There goes my bobber again! This time, you little whale, I'm going to get you." He pulled in the line quickly. . . and carefully.

There wasn't a little whale wiggling on the hook but it was a bluegill, a big bluegill, even bigger than the bluegills Grandpa had caught.

"You're right, Grandpa! I can do it if I try! I just love to fish!"

Plop! there went the red-and-white bobber on the water again.

"Oh, look, Timmy, it looks like you have another one," Grandpa said.

Timmy laughed, "Yes, I do, Grandpa. I'm learning how to be a fisherman. Someday maybe I'll be as good as you are."

Grandpa chuckled, "You probably will, Timmy. But I hope you'll be even better than I am at playing the guitar. C'mon, it's time to go home and cook these fish. And maybe you'd like to do some practicing this afternoon."

"Sure, Grandpa," said Timmy. "Just wait! Soon I'll play a special song just for you."

The Rainy Day

"Oh, no! *Not rain again!*" Billy grumbled. "I want the rain to stop NOW!"

Billy was in a not-so-very-good mood this morning. His mother called it Billy's BAD mood. It was almost Billy's VERY BAD mood.

"Well, why don't you do something fun?"

"Don't want to do anything fun. I want to go outside and swing and run and play ball."

"Read a book," said Mother.

"Don't want to read a book," said Billy.

"Watch TV," said Mother.

"Don't want to watch TV," said Billy.

Billy's BAD mood was getting worse. The corners of his mouth were turning down and down and down.

Mother put her arm around Billy and used her it's-time-to-behave voice.

"So, now you get to help me. Go upstairs this very minute, get dressed, and then clean out your messy, messy closet."

"Aw, Mom, do I have to?" Billy moaned.

"Yes, you do. And go upstairs NOW!"

Billy stomped up the steps. He didn't like rainy days at all. He liked cleaning out his closet even less.

He opened the closet door. His closet was a mess—a messy, messy mess.

Bang! he picked up a shoe and threw it out. Bang! the next shoe just missed his dog.

"Phew, these socks smell so bad. So do these old tennis shoes." Out they went with two softer bangs.

In a corner was a dusty old book.

"What's this book all about? I don't remember seeing it. It even smells dusty."

Billy opened the book to the first page.

There was some writing on the inside cover.

To our precious son
BILLY
From Mother and Father
1908

"1908? I wasn't even born until a few years ago," mumbled Billy. "Oh, now I get it. This book was given to my great grandpa Bill when he was just a little boy."

Billy carefully turned to another page. It said, "A Bible Story Book for Children."

Suddenly a wonderful world of adventure opened up for Billy—stories about kings and a giant and a chariot of fire. Then he read about a donkey who talked, a man who walked on water, and a great big net full of fish.

Billy kept turning page after page. He smiled when he read the story of the Good

Shepherd. Billy imagined that he was also hunting for a lost sheep and how happy he was when he finally found that sheep.

Billy wished he could have been one of the children who climbed on Jesus' lap.

Then he imagined he was on a mission-ary journey with the apostle Paul. It felt so good to tell people the good news about Jesus.

After the two loud BANGS and two softer bangs, Billy's mother didn't hear any noises—either soft ones or loud ones. Mother tiptoed upstairs and peeked into Billy's room. There he was, half in and half out of his closet, reading and reading and reading.

"Billy, you've been up here almost two hours. Look! the sun is shining. Now you can go outside."

"Mom, I've found the best book in my closet. It's about kings and a giant and it tells about when Jesus lived on earth, and. . . ."

"I'm glad you found something to do, Billy. And that is a very special book. Your great-grandfather read that one when he was just a boy."

Billy was in a good mood now. He was happy. The corners of his mouth curled up in a big smile.

The sun was out.

He was going to run and swing and play ball in the park.

His friends were calling him.

And he had found a special treasure while it was raining.

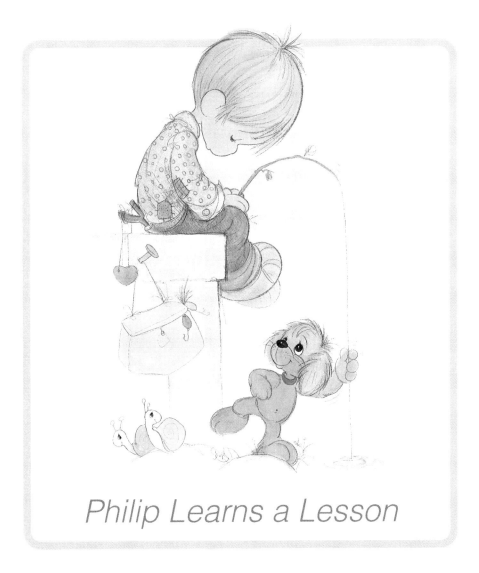

Philip Learns a Lesson

Philip and his dog Tippy left home as soon as it was light. They were off to the river to catch some big fish. But Philip was still sleepy and the bright, warm sun made Philip feel very cozy. He closed his eyes. Soon he was almost sleeping.

Tug, tug, TUG! Something was tugging at the fishing line. This wasn't just a little nibble. This fish wanted the worm and line and pole. Was it a ten-pounder?

Philip opened his eyes and shook his head. There was his bobber on top of the water. No fish! Not even a little one.

Tug, tug, TUG! TUG!

"Tippy, what are you doing?" Tippy was tugging on the line. He wanted to play.

"Oh, all right," Philip said, as he took a ball out of his fishing bag. "Let's play. I'm never going to catch anything with this crummy pole anyway. When Dad comes home tonight I'm going to tell him that I need a real fishing pole, not just a tree branch."

As soon as Dad settled down in his favorite chair, Philip plunked on the floor in front of him and said very quietly, "Dad, I have something important to talk about."

"What is it, Philip?"

Philip looked sad. "I've been using the

same crummy old branch for fishing all summer, and I never catch anything with it. I need a real pole, Dad. None of the other kids has to use a stick. Amy caught three fish yesterday with her new pole. And do you know what? Her dad bought it for her."

Father smiled as he said, "Philip, you

can have a new fishing pole any time. But you will have to buy it yourself."

"But, Dad," Philip protested, "I don't have any money!"

"I could buy that pole for you, Philip, but I'll tell you why I'm not going to. Remember that sled you just had to have last winter? You used it twice and then decided that sliding in a cardboard box was better. I think if you earn the money to buy the fishing pole yourself, you will appreciate it much more."

That night Philip made some plans. He drifted off to sleep thinking about mowing lawns and raking and weeding gardens.

After breakfast, Philip ran down to Mrs. Bronner's house to see if he could walk her dog. Mrs. Bronner was happy to see Philip and offered to pay him for exercising her dog. This was fun. Even Tippy liked the company as the three of them took a long walk and run in the woods.

Clink! there went some coins in Philip's piggy bank. But Philip needed more money, so off he went to ask the neighbors if they needed help with weeding or mowing. He was busy all morning and he had some more money to put in the bank. Clink! Clink! Poof. He even had a dollar bill to put in.

The next day was hot, too hot to work hard. "Tippy, even you are hot! I know, I'll sell some lemonade. This is just the right day for a cold drink." So, with a few hard bangs with his dad's hammer, Philip made a lemonade stand. Next, he fixed a big bowl of lemonade with ice cubes. Philip picked a spot under the maple tree and waited for customers. In just a few minutes the mailman stopped and bought two glasses. Then a grandpa and grandma came along. Soon Philip's lemonade bowl was empty, but his pockets were heavy with coins. They made lots of

clinks as they went into the piggy bank.

Philip worked hard all week. Every day more coins clinked into the piggy bank. There were even some poofs as dollar bills softly tumbled in. On Saturday Philip took all the money out of the bank and counted it. And was he surprised! There was more than enough money to buy the pole Philip wanted.

"Dad! Dad!" Philip called. "I can buy my own pole now."

"I'm proud of you, Philip," Dad said as he gave Philip a big hug.

Philip and Tippy ran all the way to the store. After they paid for the fishing pole, they stopped to get a big ice cream cone. But before Philip was able to take a lick,
PLOP!!!
the ice cream fell on the ground. Tippy made a dive for it.

Philip giggled, "Oh, well, Tippy, I guess we both got something special today."

Tippy looked up
and smiled.
And Philip had a
big smile, too.

Brian's Bear

Little Brian had a very best friend—a
soft brown bear named Teddy. Every
night Brian would pick up Teddy, climb
the stairs, and get into bed. When Mom
came in for a good-night kiss, Brian would
hold up Teddy and say, "Teddy wants a
kiss, too, Mom."

Brian and Teddy did everything together. When Brian went to the park, so did Teddy. When Brian went to the store,

Teddy came along and they rode side-by-side in the grocery cart. When Brian ate lunch, Teddy ate lunch.

Brian had a five-year-old cousin named Andy. One day Andy asked Brian to spend the night at his house. Brian was very excited and the first thing he packed was Teddy.

Brian and Andy had lots of fun. They laughed and played. All the while, Teddy was close by, watching and smiling. The boys told funny stories until way past their bedtime.

The next morning the boys jumped out of bed and ran downstairs to quickly eat breakfast and get ready to play.

The next thing they knew, Brian's mom came to pick him up. Brian ran upstairs to get Teddy. He had left him in the chair by the bed because Teddy looked so sleepy that morning. He wasn't used to sleeping in a strange house and really needed a morning nap.

Brian came running down the steps. He was crying big, big tears.

"Mom, Teddy's gone. I can't find him anywhere. He's just disappeared."

Everyone in the house looked for Teddy. They looked behind the chairs, under the bed, on all the shelves. They even looked

in the waste baskets. No Teddy, anywhere! Then they looked in the backyard.
No Teddy. There was only one place left,
the front yard. They looked under every
bush and behind every tree. Still no
Teddy.

Brian went up to the bedroom again to
see if Teddy was there. He was still crying
big tears. Andy was waiting for him.

"Brian, I have something to tell you,"
Andy said quietly. "I'm really sorry that I
made you cry."

Brian wiped his eyes. "Oh, you didn't
make me sad, Andy. I'm just sad because
I can't find my Teddy."

Andy looked down at his feet. "But I
know where Teddy is," he said. "I didn't
mean to make you cry. I have never had a
bear before and I didn't think you would
miss him that much. I'm really sorry,
Brian." And Andy began to cry.

Brian gave Andy a hug and for a few

minutes the cousins cried together. Then Andy went to the closet, pushed the shoes out of the way, pulled out a box from the corner, and lifted Teddy out of his hiding place.

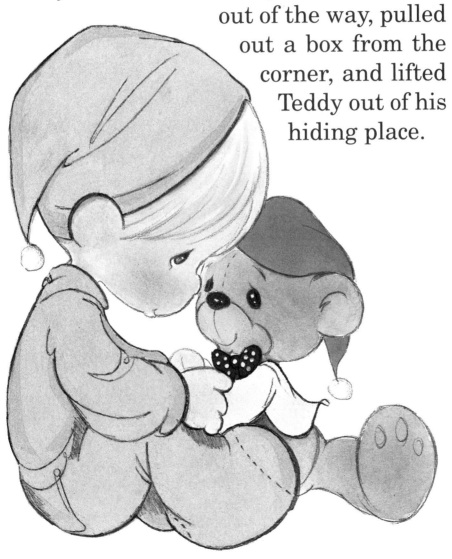

"Here he is, Brian. I did a bad thing when I took Teddy and hid him. I'm sorry. I feel so sad." Andy cried a few more tears—and these were VERY BIG TEARS. He even sobbed a few times and just kept his head down.

"That's OK, Andy, I know you didn't do it to make me sad," Brian said as he hugged Teddy.

Andy tried hard to stop crying.

Brian reached over to pat Andy's shoulder. Then he smiled and said, "I've got a good idea. Just wait here, Andy, and I'll be back in a minute."

In a few minutes Brian came back with a sheet of paper folded to make a small square. On the outside it said:

To Andy
from
Your friend Brian

Andy carefully unfolded the paper. There was a drawing of a teddy bear.

"I wish this was a real bear, Andy," Brian said, "but at least you can keep this picture until you have your very own teddy bear."

Andy giggled, "Oh, thank you, Brian. I may not need a real teddy bear. I like this picture because you made it to help me feel better."

That night when he went to bed, Andy asked his dad to hang the drawing of the teddy bear above his bed. Before he went to sleep, Andy looked up at his teddy bear and said, "'Night, Teddy, I'm so glad you came to live with me."

Animal
Tales

Me First

Rollie was a little bear who had to be first. He ALWAYS had to be first. If he was second or third, he would push his way up to the front of the line. He would push hard with his sharp elbows or give a mean shove with his shoulders.

When it was time to eat, Rollie AL-WAYS took the biggest piece. Rollie

ALWAYS helped himself first, even if his grandmother was eating with them and should have had first choice.

Rollie never shared anything—his toys, his food, or his very favorite bike. He always wanted first turn, or to be first at bat if he was playing ball. Rollie was a VERY GREEDY bear. He was not fun to be with.

One day Teddy Bear came rushing over to his friends, "C'mon!!! I've found a honey tree. It's the biggest one I've ever seen. And this is how I found it."

Of course, Rollie couldn't wait to hear the details. He waited until the others were busy talking and then ZOOM!! Rollie quietly sneaked away. He had heard just enough to find the tree and, of course, he ALWAYS had to be the first one. So when the friends got to the big tree on the hill, there was no honey, none at all. Just a very sticky Rollie.

Another day, Panda Bear came running up to the bear friends. "C'mon!!! I've just found the biggest blackberry bush in the valley. It's not far from the big pine tree. C'mon!!! I'll show you where it is."

Again, Rollie did not wait for the details. He ran as fast as his bear legs would carry him. He was out of breath when he found the blackberry bush, but that didn't stop him from pushing one berry after another in his mouth. The friends made a lot of noise scrambling through the valley but when they saw Rollie, they didn't make any noise at all. They were very quiet. Rollie had a very purple face. He had eaten all the blackberries. There wasn't even one blackberry left.

The bear friends were sitting in the sun one day when Teddy came rushing up over the hill. "C'mon!!! I know where there's a great fishing hole. It's just past the bend in the river. I just saw the biggest fish ever there!"

Would you like to guess what Rollie did? You're right. He took off for the fishing hole without waiting for the other friends. He ALWAYS had to be first.

When the bear friends rounded the

bend they saw a very unhappy Rollie. He was crying. And he didn't have any fish, either.

"What happened to you, Rollie?" asked Teddy.

Rollie wiped his eyes. "I tried to catch the biggest fish in the river. But it turned out not to be a fish at all. It was a very snappy turtle. It bit me right on the tail," Rollie sobbed.

"And that's not all, either," Rollie cried. "A big bee stung me right on the shoulder. I'm hurting all over!"

"But I knew that turtle was there, Rollie. If you had waited for us, we could have helped you and you probably wouldn't have a turtle bite and a bee sting," said Teddy.

Rollie sobbed, "If only I hadn't been so greedy. I think I've learned my lesson today. Will you still be my friends? I'll try hard not to be first all the time. But will you let me be first once in a while?"

The friends gave Rollie a big bear hug. They were glad not to have a GREEDY Rollie anymore.

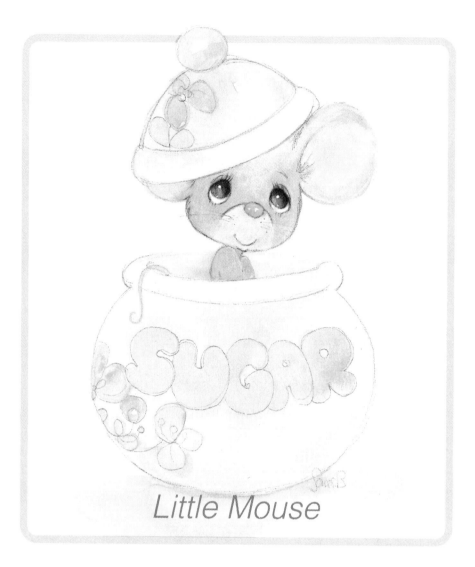

Little Mouse

Little Mouse lived in the sugar bowl on the bottom shelf of Mrs. Nagel's kitchen cupboard. He loved his home because Mrs. Nagel was such a nice lady. She always made sure Little Mouse had lots of cheese and crackers to eat. And she was quiet when Little Mouse was sleeping. Once he took a nap on a shelf. He was sleeping so soundly that he didn't hear any sounds when Mrs. Nagel came with a paintbrush to paint the shelf. She quietly painted one end of the shelf, then the other. Little Mouse slept on. She painted above him. She painted below him. Little Mouse didn't stir. She finally had to stop painting because Little Mouse kept on sleeping. Mrs. Nagel was too kind to wake him up.

But Mr. Nagel was not quiet. Mr. Nagel did not like Little Mouse. He would yell at Little Mouse and throw things at him. If he saw Little Mouse run across the floor, Mr. Nagel would jump on a chair. He even put mouse traps in the cupboards! Little Mouse had to be careful when he scampered through the cupboards. One day he was going so fast that SNAP! the tip of Little Mouse's tail was caught in the trap. Little Mouse cried and howled. But they

were only tiny noises because a mouse is not very big.

Mrs. Nagel heard Little Mouse's tiny noises. She lifted him out of the trap, bandaged his tail, put him in his sugar bowl, and gave him some cheese.

"Stay in the bowl and rest, Little Mouse," she said. "You'll feel better in the morning."

Mrs. Nagel was right. Little Mouse's tail did not hurt the next morning. But Little Mouse was still sad. You see, his heart hurt because Mr. Nagel did not like him.

Little Mouse wondered about that problem all day. He wondered so hard that he was very tired at night. He still didn't have an answer but thought there was nothing better to do but go to sleep.

Little Mouse was asleep only a short time when his nose began to twitch. It twitched and twitched. Little Mouse rubbed his paw over his nose but then he sat up straight. "I smell something. Something is hurting my nose. I think that is SMOKE."

Sure enough, when Little Mouse jumped out of his sugar-bowl home, onto the shelf, and then found his favorite track down to the floor, he knew there was smoke. He saw some FLAMES coming out of the stove.

"Oh, dear!!! Oh, dear!!! Oh, dear!!!" said Little Mouse. He would have said some more Oh-dears but there wasn't any time to lose. He ran to the bedroom and climbed up to where Mr. and Mrs. Nagel were sleeping. They were sound asleep. They didn't know their house was burning. Little Mouse jumped down on Mrs. Nagel's arm. She woke up.

"Little Mouse, Little Mouse! What are you doing here?" she cried. She was very surprised and still much too sleepy to smell smoke. Little Mouse ran up her arm and down her arm again, just to be sure she would really wake up.

Mrs. Nagel sat up. "George!!! Wake up! Wake up NOW!!! I smell smoke. Let's call the fire department and get out of here."

They both quickly climbed out of bed, called the fire department, and ran outside.

The firemen worked hard to put out the fire.

"There is only a little damage to your kitchen, Mrs. Nagel. How did you wake up in time?" the fire chief asked.

Mrs. Nagel smiled. Mr. Nagel smiled. He picked up Little Mouse. "A little friend warned us," Mr. Nagel said.

Little Mouse was so happy to hear Mr. Nagel call him a friend. Little Mouse wouldn't have to worry about traps in the cupboard anymore. In fact, Mr. Nagel gave Little Mouse a tiny little mouse hug before he put him back in the sugar bowl.

Little Mouse was a happy mouse, and he was home to stay.

Leo's Birthday

Today is Leo's birthday. He is five years old today. All his life he had lived at the circus. When he was a little cub, crowds of people would come to see him puff out his chest and try to roar. It wasn't a roar at all, just a soft, baby noise. But Leo grew and grew. Soon he had big teeth and could ROAR like a big lion. But all the people knew Leo had a soft heart and was just acting. When the crowds went home, Leo would roll over and purr until someone rubbed his big furry tummy. Everyone loved Leo.

Leo's friend Duncan was so sad. "Today is Leo's birthday," he said. "And I don't have a present for him. I wanted to make something nice. All I have are some tools and an old rug. I can't make a present out of that."

Leo's other friend Bambi

was also sad. He said, "Today is Leo's birthday. And I don't have a present for him. I wanted to make something nice, but all I have is some boards and paint. I can't make a present out of this."

Duncan heard Bambi's sad story. "Let's cooperate," said Duncan.

"What's cooperate?" asked Bambi.

"It's when we work together to get something done," Duncan said. "If we put our stuff together, we can make something much nicer than we could make alone."

Duncan and Bambi decided to cooperate. Bambi held the boards while Duncan sawed them. Bambi brushed pretty red paint on the boards while Duncan held the paint can. And while Duncan was putting his rug on the new floor, Bambi was hanging curtains in the window.

When they were finished, Duncan and Bambi stood back.

"That's a beautiful lion house!" Bambi said.

"We did it right because we worked together," Duncan replied.

And the two happy friends went off to find Leo. They made him shut his eyes as they led him toward the present they had made.

"OK, now you may open your eyes," Bambi said. "Turn around, Leo. Here's a

present we made for your fifth birthday.
We wanted to make something special for
you."

"Wow!!!" said Leo. "My very own lion house. And you painted it my favorite color. This is the best present I ever had. Thanks, friends. You made my day."

*School
Days*

Marcia's Beautiful Voice

Marcia had a beautiful voice. But Marcia had a problem. She was TOO PROUD of her beautiful voice.

"My, you have a nice voice, Marcia," her friends would say.

"I know it," Marcia would reply. "I'm going to be the world's best singer."

One day Marcia's friends were reading a poster in the school hallway.

"What's that all about?" Marcia asked.

"Oh, Marcia," Mary replied, "there's going to be a singing contest tomorrow night. You'll just have to be there."

"Is that so? I'll probably win the contest because I'm the best singer around, but I guess I could enter," Marcia quipped.

During class the music teacher asked Bryan to hand out yellow cards with the contest rules. When he offered Marcia one, she turned up her nose and said. "I don't need one of those stupid cards! Everyone knows that I have the best voice. I'm going to win that contest without even trying to."

"Why didn't you take the rule card, Marcia?" Tammy asked as they waited their turn to perform. "Some of the rules weren't about singing."

"Who needs rules?" snapped Marcia. "Rules are made for people who can't sing."

"Well, here I go," said Tammy. "I'll do my best but I don't think I'm going to win."

"I hope you have just a short song to sing," snapped Marcia. "This contest is taking so-o-oo long."

Marcia was last in line and was very impatient about waiting for her turn.

"Will that Jenny ever finish?" she complained. "Just listen to her! How did she ever get into this contest with a crummy voice like that?"

"Jenny has a nice voice," Tammy argued.

"Well, of course, *you* would think so," snapped Marcia. "After all, you never had a voice lesson in your life."

After waiting for a very long time, Marcia was called to center stage. *I'm*

terrific! she thought to herself as she sang
with her nose high in the air.

"You were wonderful," said Tammy.

"It's like they always say," Marcia boasted. "We save the best for last."

"Well, I think you should tell Jenny that you're sorry you said she had a crummy voice," insisted Tammy.

"OK, I'm sorry that your voice is crummy, Jenny," Marcia laughed as she looked at Jenny.

Tears ran down Jenny's cheeks. Marcia just chuckled again.

Suddenly the music teacher walked on stage. Everyone, except Marcia, wondered who the winner would be. Marcia knew that Marcia would win.

"Ladies and gentlemen, we have a winner. Jenny Bronson, will you please come up?" said the teacher.

The audience clapped loudly.

Marcia gasped and looked at Jenny with surprise.

"As you know," the teacher continued, "to be a great singer one must have more than just a nice voice. One must have a friendly smile and poise and a pleasing personality. Jenny meets all of these qualifications. Congratulations, Jenny! You are the winner."

The audience clapped again. Jenny smiled and smiled. No one noticed that there were dried tears on her cheeks.

"Where's Marcia?" Jenny asked as soon as she joined her friends.

"I think she found the losers' corner," Tammy quipped.

"Let's go find her," said Jenny. "She must be feeling very sad."

"Marcia, I'm so sorry," Jenny said when she found Marcia. "I know you were counting on winning."

"I'm sorry, too," cried Marcia. "But not because I lost, Jenny. I'm sorry because I was so proud and so mean to you. I'm

going to try to have a beautiful personality like you do. That's more important than having a beautiful voice."

And all the friends clapped loudly as Jenny put her arms around her friend Marcia.

Being Different Is Special

Jim waved good-bye to his school friends as his mother drove up in the station wagon.

"How was school today?" Mother asked as she pulled away from the curb.

"OK. I did really good on my science test." Jim showed her the paper with the happy face drawn on it.

"Very good, Son, an A! I'm proud of you and Dad will be, too. Anything else happen today?"

"Well, we played kick ball at recess time. That was a blast!"

Mother laughed as she looked at the dirt on Jim's jeans. "I can see that you had a lot of fun."

"Yeah, we sure did, all of us except Michael."

"Who is Michael?" Mother asked.

"He's a new boy at school. Some of the kids were making fun of him and he started crying."

"Why were the other kids picking on him?" Mother asked.

"He has to use crutches. Sometimes he needs help walking."

"Jim, I want to ask you something. What kind of a boy do you think Michael would be if he didn't need crutches?"

Jim thought for a minute as he looked out the window. "Just like the rest of us, I guess."

"Now, what if your legs didn't work right? What if they were weak and you had to use crutches?" asked Mother.

"Well, my legs might be weak, but I would have strong arms and eyes and ears and my brain would be like anyone else's."

"How about your feelings, Jim? Would you like to have people tease you about your weak legs? Or to laugh at you because you walked differently?"

"No, Mom, I wouldn't."

Mother smiled at Jim and said, "Everyone of us is a little bit different."

"I'm glad we're different, Mom. I mean, you like to grow flowers and bake cookies. I like to eat cookies and watch the stars and planets."

"It wouldn't be very much fun if we were

all the same," agreed Mother. "Being different makes you special. And you are very special, Jim. So is Michael."

"Now I know why Michael cried," Jim said. "He's just like the rest of us, except for his legs. Some people have weak eyes, or weak ears. But that doesn't give us the right to tease them."

"Right, Son," said Mother. "Some people can't hear well, some people have trouble talking clearly. Some people can't walk. Some people can't see. We are all different, each of us in our own way."

Jim thought about that for a minute or two. Suddenly he turned to Mother and said, "Stop, Mom. There's Michael now. He sure looks sad climbing those steps. I'll see if he can come over to our house. Tom and John are coming to work on pinebox derby cars. Michael can make one, too."

"Hey, Michael!" Jim called. "Can you

come over and work on pinebox derby cars? Tom and John are coming, too. We can have a mock race as soon as we're finished."

Michael smiled as he shuffled over to the car. "I'd like that, Jim. Last year I made a couple of cars and almost won the derby. I think if I make one or two changes, I'll have a sure winner this time."

"Good," said Jim. "See you soon. You can probably give us some good tips because this is our first year in the derby."

As he turned to his mom, Jim said, "Let's get going. I hope you have lots of chocolate chip cookies, Mom, because derby racers get really hungry!"

Clown School

Did you know that clowns have to go to school to learn how to juggle, and balance, and put on their sad or happy faces?

Boomer and Taffy had been clowns for a long time and now they were teachers at the Happy Day Clown School.

"Boomer!" Taffy called. "You'd better

hurry. You don't want to be late for the first day of school."

Boomer grabbed his lunch box and hurried after his friend. "I wonder what kind of clowns we'll have to teach this year," he said.

Taffy laughed. "Well, they can't be as bad as last year's clowns! Do you remember little Flip and his Amazing Wonder Dog? Flip tried everything to get that puppy to do his tricks. And then there was Topper, the world's clumsiest clown! He wanted to be a juggler but the balls kept landing on his head."

"And who could forget little Beanie?" giggled Boomer. "She wanted to be the best roller skating clown ever.

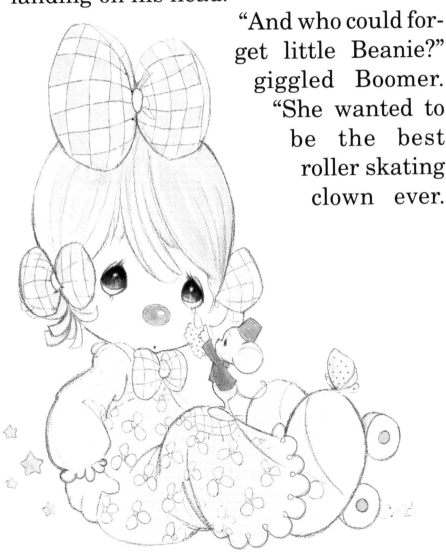

The only problem was that she couldn't stay up for more than two minutes. By the end of the third week we had pillows tied all over her to keep her safe."

Taffy giggled again. "Do you remember Lolly and Pop, her goose? Lolly tried to train that silly thing to walk the tightrope, but all the goose wanted to do was eat her bows and ribbons. Wasn't Lolly surprised when Pop turned out to be the best high diver the circus ever had?"

"Yes," said Boomer, "Lolly turned out to be a very good tightrope walker! I think that's what I like best about being a teacher. We start out every year with a bunch of little clowns who fall all over each other trying to be the best clown. But by the end of the year the little clowns realize that when they work together and help each other, each clown can discover what he or she can do the best."

"That's right," Taffy agreed. "When Flip tried to teach Topper how to juggle without dropping the balls, Flip discovered he could catch just about anything. Now Flip is our best juggler."

"And if Topper didn't try to help Beanie learn to balance," said Boomer, "Topper wouldn't have discovered how good he is on the unicycle. I don't think I've ever seen anyone who can do the tricks he does. . . and he was our clumsiest clown."

As Boomer and Taffy walked through the school gates, they saw all kinds of little clowns tumbling and falling all over each other.

"Oh, well," Boomer laughed, "here we go again."

The Faker

"I don't like school!" Timmy groaned as he turned over in bed. He stuck a fever thermometer in his mouth, hoping he was sick.

"Shucks, no fever today," sighed Timmy. "Guess I'll have to get up."

Timmy stomped out of the bedroom. Then he tramped down the steps, plunk,

plunk!! PLUNK!!!! And he was just as noisy coming into the kitchen. He got himself some juice out of the refrigerator.

He grumped at the refrigerator, snarled at the stove, and glared at the bread dough and flour on the kitchen counter. He really did like Mom's homemade bread, but he was much too crabby to think about that.

Seeing all that white flour on the counter gave Timmy an idea. It was such a good idea that he almost smiled.

"Let's see, if I plan this right, I won't have to go to school today," Timmy said aloud to no one in particular.

Timmy sneaked over to the counter, picked up two handfuls of flour, and rubbed the flour all over his face. He didn't notice that he had a collar of white flour and smears of white flour all over his arms. There was even a clump or two of flour in his hair.

"Wow! I must really look sick now."

A few minutes later, Timmy's mother walked into the room. She saw Timmy holding his stomach and moaning. She also saw the clumps of flour in Timmy's hair and the smears of flour on his cheeks and chin. Mother covered up a smile and tried to look sad.

"Oh, Timmy!" Mother cried. "What is wrong with you?"

"I'm so sick this morning, Mom, that I just can't even think of going to school," Timmy groaned.

"Well, I had better get your father!" Mother cried.

When Timmy's father saw how white he was, he shook his head sadly. "Poor, poor Timmy!" he said.

"Poor Timmy is sick," his mother said, trying to hide her smile. "Look at how white he is. Do you think he has the flu?"

"How horrible! How sad!" Father said.

"Maybe you should cook some eggs and send him back to bed as soon as he is finished eating. You know," his father continued, "I once read that eggs with plenty of pepper is the best thing to cure the flu."

"That's true," said Mother as she put two eggs on Timmy's plate.

"And now for the best part," Father said as he secretly winked at Mother.

Father took the pepper shaker and began to cover Timmy's eggs with pepper. All at once, Timmy's nose began to twitch and he let out a great big sneeze.

"Ker-choo!"
"KER-CHOO-OO!!!"

Flour flew in all directions and began to settle on the kitchen floor.

Timmy's face no longer was white. Even the clumps of flour in his hair had disappeared. There were only a few streaks of flour on his shoulders, and they didn't make Timmy look at all sick.

"Well, what do you know? It worked," Timmy's father laughed. "Now, Timmy, it looks like all the flu bugs have left. You just lost your excuse for missing school today."

Timmy's face turned all shades of red. He was so ashamed that he forgot to feel sorry that his trick didn't work.

Father said, "There is a verse in the Bible that says, 'Be sure your sin will find you out.' That verse means that sooner or later the wrong things that we do will be discovered and then we will be sorry that we sinned. And I would say that your little plan to stay home from school didn't work, Tim."

Timmy gulped. "But your trick on me worked, didn't it?"

Mother smiled as she dusted the flour

from Timmy's pajama top. "You know," she said, "Father and I knew what you were up to, Timmy. But rather than talking to you or scolding you about it, we wanted to find out if our trick would teach you a lesson you wouldn't forget."

"It sure was a good lesson, Mom. I'm sorry that I tried to trick you."

"And now that you are feeling so much better, don't you think it's time to get ready for school?" Mother suggested.

Field Day

"Oh, boy!!! Today is Field Day," yelled Ricky as he climbed out of bed. He was excited about the big race. He always won and that made him very happy.

There were races, long jumps, and all sorts of other sports on Field Day. Ricky's friends were going to be in the races, too. And parents and grandparents always came. There were lots of people to cheer and lots of people to hug the winners. Sometimes grandmas and grandpas had to comfort the losers, but Ricky didn't even want to think about that.

Ricky got to school early that day. Kids were on the playground and teachers began to line up the children so Field Day could begin.

The first event was the softball throw. Girls and boys threw softballs as far as they could, and the teachers measured how far each ball went.

Ricky's friend Jimmy had thrown the best toss so far. Now it was Ricky's turn. His teacher handed him the softball. The ball felt good in his hand. He looked at Mom and Dad and smiled. Then he wound up and th-r-e-w-w-w with all his might. Never had Ricky thrown a ball so far. It sailed through the air and landed with a hard thud. His classmates cheered. Ricky had thrown the ball beyond the mark made by Jimmy. Ricky won that toss, but not by much.

Next came the broad jump. They stood at the line and jumped as far as they could. One by one the children lined up and jumped. Sure enough, Jimmy jumped way beyond everyone else. It looked like Jimmy was going to win this one. Now it was Ricky's turn. He jumped farther than anyone else, just a little bit farther than Jimmy did. So Ricky won that contest. And Jimmy came in second.

The final event of the day was the 50-yard dash. This was the most important race. And, of course, Ricky wanted to win. So did Jimmy. The friends looked at each

other and smiled. Each knew that the other one could beat him. But both of them were going to try hard to win.

"On your mark!"

"Get set!"

"GO-o-o-oo!"

Ricky quickly took the lead, running as fast as his legs could carry him. The others fell behind, except for Jimmy, who was running very fast, too. Suddenly the friends were even. The two best friends were tied with only a few more feet to go. They were huffing and puffing! Everyone was cheering them on. Then Jimmy took the lead. Jimmy had won! Jimmy had finally won a race. He just smiled and smiled. Then, with his hands high in the air, he began jumping up and down with happiness!!!

But Ricky, who had never lost a race, wasn't happy at all. He was very UN-happy. He began to cry.

"I'm sorry, Mom and Dad," Ricky whimpered.

"Son, there is nothing to be sorry about," said his father. "You did a fine job."

"Sure," his mother agreed. "You've had your day in the sun, which is more than some people ever get."

Ricky looked at his mom and said, "What do you mean by 'day in the sun,' Mom?"

"You've won many events and most people don't win even one. Finishing second isn't bad. You don't have to feel sorry about that. The idea is to have fun and be happy for the winner."

"You're right, Mom," said Ricky. "I've got to go over and congratulate Jimmy now."

Both of the best-friend winners had big smiles.

"Congratulations, Jimmy. You're the best!" said Ricky.

"Congratulations yourself, Ricky. I think you're the best," said Jimmy.

And the best friends went off the field together, arms around each other's shoulders.

*Sleepytime
Stories*

Sweet Dreams

Tommy said his prayers and climbed into bed. His mom had told him to think of nice things before he went to sleep so he could have sweet dreams.

With a big smile on his face, Tommy stretched out, put his hands under his head, and said, "Let's see, what's the first thing I want to do tomorrow?"

It was butterfly time where Tommy lived. Maybe Tommy and his friend Scott could watch the butterflies in the open field next to Tommy's house. Scott and Tommy together had counted over a hundred butterflies there yesterday.

"Just think," said Scott. "These butterflies used to be yukky caterpillars. Now they're flying fast through the air. They've forgotten about being caterpillars."

Tommy's eyes began to close. He dreamed he was a butterfly and the soft wind was carrying him across the field. Whoops!! he landed on a mushroom, a blue one!

Tommy was growing tired of being on the mushroom. *Maybe I'll turn myself back into Tommy and watch the ants for a while. I just love to see them scurrying around. They're always so-oo-o busy.* So he headed for the big anthill. Tommy's mother had told him that ants were the strongest insects in the world. He believed that, because he watched them carry sand around. They were hurrying around the anthill, each one busy doing his job. Tommy stayed for about ten minutes and then decided he had watched the ants long enough.

Dianne, Tommy's sister, had found some baby birds that day. She even held one that had fallen from its nest. But, of course, Dianne wouldn't let Tommy hold it. She was the big sister and Tommy was only a little boy—much too little to know how to hold a baby bird!

Hah!!! Now I'll be able to hold that little bird. Maybe I can even hold two birds! Tommy was really having a good dream this time. When Tommy finally found the nest, Mama Bird was guarding the two little ones and wouldn't let Tommy get near them, not even in his dream.

Now what will I dream about? Hmmm, I'm beginning to smell pancakes and bacon and yummy cinnamon rolls. I sure hope this isn't a dream—because I'm very hungry.

"Tommy! Tommy! It's time to get up! Breakfast is ready and waiting," called Mother. "Did you have sweet dreams last night?"

What do you think Tommy said?

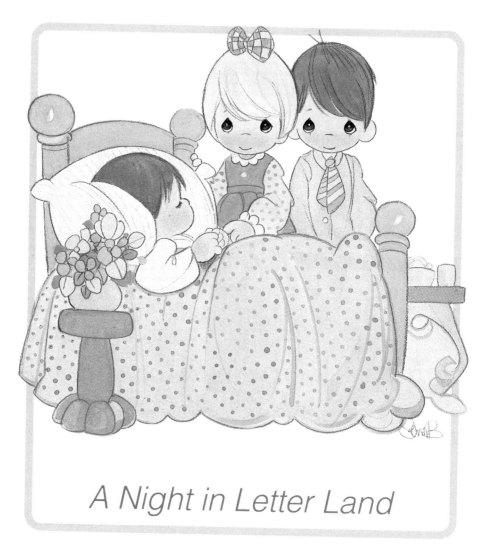

A Night in Letter Land

Benji didn't like to do his homework, and he especially hated to work on spelling. He thought it was silly to learn how to make the letters of the alphabet into words.

"Why do I have to learn the alphabet or how to spell?" he complained to his parents. "I want to be a baseball player, and they don't have to know the ABCs to hit a ball."

"Everyone needs to know the ABCs or they will get into trouble," Mother said. "But right now it's time to S-L-E-E-P. Good night!"

"'Night, M-O-M! 'Night, D-A-D!" Benji said as he turned over and closed his eyes.

BING! ! BING! Two strange characters were suddenly standing by Benji's bed.

"Who are you?" asked Benji.

"We are A to Z," Mr. A said. "And we have come to tell you how much you need us."

"What makes you think *I* need *you?*" Benji snapped.

"Well, you see," answered Mr. A, "without us you could have a lot of problems. But before I say more, I want you to meet my friends."

Soft music played while letters of every kind hopped down from nowhere and stood by Benji's bed.

"Wow," gasped Benji. "You sure have a lot of friends."

"That's right," said Mr. A. "And you need all of us to help you in your life."

Suddenly there was a loud GROWL!

"What's that?" asked Mrs. Z.

"It's just my stomach. I forgot to eat a bedtime snack and now I'm very hungry," Benji answered.

"That's too bad," replied Mr. A. "Would you like to have some C-A-T food?"

"Well, I guess so," said Benji, who had no idea what C-A-T food was.

Snap! Mr. A snapped his fingers and a big bowl of cat food appeared.

"Yuk! that's terrible!" yelled Benji.

"Oh," said Mr. A, "we're sorry, but you see we're not people and we don't know what kind of food you eat."

"Well, I don't eat cat food," Benji huffed.

"Then what would you like?" asked Mr. A.

"I want a hot dog," answered Benji. "And hurry, please. I'm very hungry."

"Can you spell it?" asked Mr. A.

"Spell it? Why do I have to spell it?" Benji asked.

Mr. A smiled and began to explain. "You see, Benji, in our land we cannot grant a request until you spell the thing you ask for. It may seem strange to you, but that's the law of Letter Land."

"Look," Benji complained, "I'm hungry and I want my hot dog NOW!"

"And you can have it," answered Mr. A. "If you know how to spell it."

"Maybe I can, and maybe I can't," Benji growled.

"But you must try," Mr. A replied.

"OK, then, let's see now," Benji said. "I think it begins with F. Yes, that's right. It's F-A-T. Now for the word *dog* . . . um . . . er, yes, I'm sure it's H-O-G."

Another snap of Mr. A's fingers and instantly a huge hog stood in front of Benji.

"A hog???" Benji cried. "But I didn't ask for a hog."

"Oh, but you did!" replied Mr. A. "That's what you spelled."

"Okay, that's it! Now, I'm *really* mad. I want to go home right now!" Benji shouted.

"Home?" asked Mrs. Z. "And how do you spell *home?*"

"Oh, No!!!" groaned Benji. "I forgot that I have to spell out everything I need. I don't even know how to spell *home.*"

"Then. . .it looks like we have a BIG PROBLEM," said Mr. A. "Are you sure you can't spell *home?*"

"No!!! I really can't," cried Benji. "What am I going to do?"

"Maybe Mr. Bookworm can help us," suggested Mrs. Z. She gently knocked on the door of a house that looked like a dictionary. Soon a little worm opened the door.

"Good day, Mr. Bookworm," said Mrs. Z. "We are having a problem and I wonder if you can help us."

"Please, Mr. Bookworm," Benji said, "*I really am in trouble.* Can you help me?"

"As a matter of fact, I can," replied Mr. Bookworm. "But I won't!"

"You won't?" cried Benji. "Why?"

"Why should I? Spelling means nothing to you. You hate the alphabet, and you don't even want to learn," Mr. Bookworm snapped.

Tears began to fall down Benji's cheeks.

"I know," Benji said. "I really have been stubborn. But now I can see how important all of you and spelling are to me."

Mr. Bookworm looked at the alphabet letters. "Miss E, would you please come here? Oh, yes, and you too, Mrs. O and Mr. M. Now, Miss H, please stand here by me."

Each letter came quickly and stood by Mr. Bookworm.

"Suppose I did spell *home* for you." Mr. Bookworm said to Benji. "Then what happens tomorrow? Will you forget everything that happened here?"

"Oh, no, Sir!" Benji promised. "I will never forget what happened."

Mr. Bookworm could see that Benji intended to keep his promise.

"Miss H, please stand here. Mrs. O, stand between Miss H and Mr. M. Now, Miss E, please stand on the other side of Mr. M," said Mr. Bookworm.

All the letters lined up and Mr. Bookworm looked through his very thick glasses at Benji. "Benji, do you promise to remember what you have learned in Letter Land?"

"Yes, I promise," said Benji. "I will never forget and I promise always to do my homework—without grumbling."

Mr. Bookworm smiled and gave Benji a gentle hug.

"Okay, letters, let's spell H-O-M-E together, shall we?"

"Benji! Benji! It's time to wake up," Mother called.

"Wha. . .er. . .Ah. . .Mom, is that you? Well, what do you know? I'm home! HURRAY!!! HURRAY!!!"

"Did I hear you spell something?" Mother asked.

"You sure did, Mom. From now on I will be spelling every day. I spent last night in Letter Land. While I was there I really learned a L-E-S-S-O-N," Benji said as he began to get ready for school.

A Friend for Fluffy

Four-year-old Terri got a very special birthday present—a little baby kitten. Terri named the kitten Fluffy because he had a fluff of fur around his neck.

Terri and Fluffy did everything to-gether. When Terri was eating, Fluffy would sit under the table and play with Terri's shoestrings. At night, Fluffy would